To Silvester
   Best wishes

Mark. D. Tingay

20 th May.

GW00504253

SCIENCE FICTION
STORIES

SCIENCE FICTION STORIES

Mark David Tingay

Aurora Books
Sussex, England

Aurora Books
is an imprint of
the The Book Guild Ltd

Aurora Books
25 High Street,
Lewes, Sussex

First published 1992
Mark David Tingay 1992
Set in Baskerville
Typesetting by APS, Salisbury, Wiltshire
Printed in Great Britain by
Antony Rowe Ltd.
Chippenham, Wiltshire.

A catalogue record for this book is
available from the British Library

ISBN 0 86332 714 1

CONTENTS

To D Betts, Pat Tyler, Jane Hoare, Lisa Tingay, Shirley Tingay and Ron Tingay.

The Spore

Spores. These are little walled cells, suspended in animation, which drift in outer space and the entire solar system. Arrhenius spoke of a tiny particled cell drifting through space for many centuries and perhaps even longer, suspended in a time matrix. Waiting for the right moment to spore, these then drift apart from their mother bond, and then push into an occupied world. We learned from Arrhenius that spores, or the spore, couldn't survive for long out in the solar system because of the many harmful bacteria and also the sun's rays. But what would happen if a different spore was created, a spore that could withstand heat and severe cold? This would be the start of a living nightmare, and then when would it end? Would it be the destruction of all living things, throughout the different galaxies?

This is one such story, the start of a living nightmare. It started one sunny day. John Hudson was busy mowing the lawn outside in his garden, when suddenly a crack of thunder was heard. John said this can't be right, it's a bright day without a cloud in the sky, then as he glanced up he felt something land on his face. When he tried to rub it off it was strange, it wouldn't come off, then as he tried rubbing some more, he felt it pulsate under the pressure. Then, John took his hand away from his face, and dashed inside his house to see hat was causing this. When he got inside, he ran up the hall stairs, accidentally tripping over one of them. When he fell, his face was pressed up against the hall mirror. As he looked in the mirror, his face had changed into a ball of red boils, and he began to scream in panic.

While he was shouting and screaming, his next-door neighbours were watching television. The film they were watching was called *It Came from Outer Space*. They had just turned it off when they heard an almighty bang next-door. Ron said, "Did

7

you hear that, Anne?"

"Hear what, Ron?"

"That noise next door."

Anne said, "You must have been hearing things."

Then, as he put his ear to the front-room wall, he heard it again only this time it was louder and then it gave out a screech. When Ron heard this, he was scared but baffled as well so he walked round to see what it was. Anne ran after him and shouted to him not to get involved. He rang the bell, there was no answer, so he tried it again, still no answer so he trotted round and opened the back door, where he was met by the most horrific sight he had ever seen. The remains of a body skin was laid out on the grass, covered in blood, then as Anne ran up she screamed and pointed.

Then as John looked up a mass of flesh was pulsating. When he saw this his first reaction was to run, but he was glued to the spot. Then, in a split second, the organism flew at John. He tried getting out of the way, but it was no good, the thing had latched on to him. As he stood there in total panic watching this thing start to crawl up his body, the thing expanded then leapt into the air. As the organism dropped down, its body at this stage was twice as large.

When Anne saw this, she shouted to him to run. But he couldn't, he was mesmerized by it, then, as it landed on him again, this time it began devouring his inner structure. He shouted, "Help me Anne!" She fainted on the lawn, and when a couple of seconds had passed the organism had finished devouring John and now was crawling along the floor to Anne.

When Anne awoke, she saw the thing crawling up her legs. She screamed, the thing started to devour her legs in a frenzied way. When she felt this, she died of heart failure. When the organism got no response, her structure was pulped and devoured in one mouthful as the thing was gobbling and chewing. After a couple of seconds had passed, the organism just laid on the lawn pulsating, then as the temperature rose, the sun's ultra-violet rays started to mingle with the organism.

The organism seemed to grow in strength. While it was pulsating with every second, it was collecting as much heat as it could from the sun's rays. Then, as it had collected all the energy that it needed, it started moving along the path towards the street. After a couple of seconds had passed, the organism had reached the street.

A woman passed by, as she glanced down at it she let out a piercing scream. When the other people heard this they came running towards her. The organism leapt into the air and they all scattered in fright. While it was hovering up in the sky, it was looking for the easiest prey to swoop on.

A man on the ground had tripped over with all the panic, and the organism dropped down onto him, and started to devour him as he screamed in agony. Then as the organism had devoured half, the man's head leant over to one side, as blood was seen coming from his mouth. As the organism was devouring the rest of the body, its structure was increasing with every mouthful, with the brain it was eating as well. But this didn't mean that the brain was being eaten whole. Its information was first extracted and stored for future use, so it was becoming very intelligent as it was eating. Suddenly it stopped in its tracks, and when the people saw this they stopped running.

When the people who had been frantically running away had stopped, they became enthralled by the strange phenomenon, which at this time was as still as a mouse. While they were watching, all of them glanced at each other in total fear of what it might do.

Then the organism began to speak, saying to them, "Your world is finished, resistance is no good, submit yourselves to me at once, I want your brain-power."

One of the people said, "Is this the end of the world as we know it? Could it be the start of a living nightmare? Or will this organism suspend us into living spores to reproduce itself in the coming of its ultimate nightmare. The man-spores, tiny little creatures existing in their pond of unknown dimensions, and captured in time. What will the world look like in years to come?"

Then the spore spoke, saying, "I live."

This is the account of that fateful day. Could there be a second spore? Who knows.

Forgotten Shade

This tale is about an ancient shade, which was presumed lost and thought to have been sunk with the ship that was bringing it. This ship was a three-mast vessel called the *Almighty Thunder*. The story begins in a little town in Gibraltar. This town was one of these little coastal areas, where nothing out of the ordinary happens – this is what we were led to believe. Then, one wet and foggy night with a force-nine gale out at sea, a stranger walked into town. He went past one of their old lantern's, which at that moment was out of order, but as the stranger walked by it the lantern came on. While the locals were looking outside at the state of the weather, they noticed this strange happening, and looked at each other in disbelief and amazement.

Then he started looking left and right to see where he was. When the locals saw this they knew he wasn't from the area. The stranger went over to one of the houses and started to knock on the door, the sound vibrating through the house. As the local opened the door, a flash of lightning hit it and made an indentation on the door. The mark was that of the Devil. The stranger unmasked himself, and as he did so, a flash came from his eyes. It was similar to that of a negative photograph. The local closed his eyes due to the brightness of the flash, then in a split second he opened them again.

When he did so the stranger was gone. As the local looked round he was nowhere to be seen, all he saw was the open door with the rain pouring in. So he ran out of the door, in a frantic state of mind, shouting out loud as he went that he had seen the Devil and that they were doomed. When the other locals heard this, they all ran down to see what the commotion was about. As they reached this old house, which had been derelict for some time, they saw a man kneeling on the ground, praying to himself, saying over and over again "Help me God." When they saw this, one of them tried shaking him out of it. But it was no good, his face was paralyzed with fright. The other local said, "Whoever did this was not normal."

Then as the local came away from the man and turned around, he saw the man looking up into space with an expression of stupid amazement. His name was Tom Court, a man who was well-respected and well thought of in the town until now. The other local who came up to Tom was John Darkin, a well-known fisherman in the town. The gale was getting worse, even the ships anchored in the cove were feeling the force. Suddenly one of the ships had worked loose from its moorings on the dock area, its name was the *Almighty Thunder*. When the people saw this, they panicked and ran down to the dock where the ship had been tied.

While the *Almighty Thunder* was drifting out to sea, the rest of the ships had been rocked so much that their moorings were working loose. As the fisherman saw this he grabbed hold of the rope, and grappled with it as it sliced through his hands making deep indentations. When the others saw this they each grabbed a line, to ensure that the other ships did not drift out to sea.

The gale was growing in strength to force ten, so blustery that it was causing havoc in the dock area, where the locals were forcing down the ropes. When John Darkin tightened the loose rope around the point, he went to help the rest of them with the other ropes. Then as he glanced up from securing the other ropes he saw the *Almighty Thunder*, bobbing up and down in the sea.

So he said to the rest of them, "Get all your boats, we are going after the *Almighty Thunder*."

As the locals set off for their boats John was left glancing out to sea. "Whatever is out there, God help us."

He walked over to his boat, which was anchored near the shore line. As he got in it and started up, the others were at this stage about fifty yards in front of him, so he set off behind them. While the others were motoring along, a dead calm came over the sea as if it were trying to tell us something, a warning to stay away from the *Almighty Thunder*. When John had caught up with the rest of the locals, they had positioned themselves about thirty feet away from the ship, because a huge fog was in front of them.

11

While they were waiting, John got impatient and motored into the fog. When the others saw this they shouted to him to come back from the brink. But it was no good, he had made up his mind to go into the fog with no holds barred, and forgetting all the consequences. When he had gone through halfway, as the locals were watching on the outside, a giant light came out of the sky. When this happened the local people began to get frightened, then it zoomed down and started to twist around the fog with an accelerated pace. The locals started their boats and rushed off in frantic panic back to the shore, leaving poor old John Darkin behind to contend with the beast.

While all this was going on outside, John Darkin was just coming up to the ship as he drifted alongside, as he went to touch the rope ladder to get up on to the ship. The ship was cold as ice. As John Darkin felt this he drew his hand away as fast as possible, in case he got frost-bite. Then as he tied some old cloth around his hands, to get a firm grip on the rope, he was just in the process of climbing up when he heard a strange gurgling coming from beneath the boat he was in. He stopped his engines and listened some more to this strange noise, then he bent over the boat to have a clearer listen.

Then in a split second, a hand came out of the sea holding a sword. Its glittering glow was piercing to the eyes and very painful. As this came out, the *Almighty Thunder* roared with evil. When John Darkin heard this he hesitated over getting on to the ship, then in a flash the sword was released from the hand. It was hovering over the sea, towards the boat where John was. John stepped back in total amazement, then as it was just on the verge of entering the boat, for some strange reason it held back. John wondered if this could be an omen of some kind.

Then while the sword was hovering near the boat, in that second it fell into the sea with an almighty splash. After it had sunk without trace, John wondered if it was a mirage or just a big dream. His face glanced round to the ship, which was alive with noises and figures. John couldn't believe what he was witnessing. Then as he was looking up at the ship, something was moving down below. He glanced down at the sea and to his surprise the sea around him was receding, it was making way for a huge mountain which was breaking through the sea. His boat was flung into the air. John was forced against the deck of his boat, due to the magnetic thrust that had thrown him and his boat. When they descended, their point of entry was the plateau on the top of the mountain.

The coldness that he was feeling was abnormal, then in a couple of seconds John was turned into a block of ice. The boat bounced off one of the mountain's ridges and crash-landed in a small cove. When the boat crashed, John's frozen body was thrown from the boat as it descended, and came crashing down onto the plateau. John's frozen body skimmed across the ground and ended up in the middle of a canyon. As he came to a stop, the earth around him started to sink. Then after a couple of seconds, the block of ice was sinking beyond belief, then it fell deep down into the mountain's core. When the block of ice was falling very fast down this form of rounded tunnel, its presence was magnetic. It was drawing an audience of old faces past and present as it descended. The faces were echoing, saying "So you thought you had forgotten the shade?"

Then the block of ice came to a stop. It had landed in a marsh, and the temperature was cold at the start, now at boiling point as the ice floated around in the marsh. The temperature was increasing with every second, then as the block lay there, it started to melt until finally John was floating on his own.

After a couple of seconds, John came to out of his ice cabin, then as he opened his eyes to see where he was, he had the shock of his life. As he stood upright, and began spitting out the sea water that was in his mouth, he began glancing round him as he was getting out of the marsh. He tripped and went under the water as he submerged again, and felt something tight around his legs. He put his hands down to free himself, felt a cold sensation, and as he lifted them out of the water his hands had been chewed off. When John saw this, he screamed then fainted. The marsh had receded and the cave around him was alight with bright lights and white figures.

When John awoke out of his state, the pain had gone and when he looked down at his hands they had been restored to full working order. A voice spoke from above, it said we have mended your hands. Then it said, "But be warned, if you go now all will be forgiven, but if you don't, God help you."

Below him in the water something was stirring, making a deafening noise. As John put his hand down into the receding water, the figures above him said, "No, it is forbidden to reach down a second time."

When John heard this he still went on, and a huge golden shade surfaced and said, "So you are the one that seeks me."

John shouted with joy, then said, "Yes, I am the one."

The shade turned around and looked up at the figures. "I will transport you back to the *Almighty Thunder*."

John said, "No, I won't go."

But it was too late, he was on his way, through the time barriers and beyond the unknown mysteries of life. When he came to he found himself on the *Almighty Thunder* which at this stage was going into port. When John saw this he said to himself, "Was it a dream, or was the shade real, I will never know."

Then, as the ship came into dock, it roared then turned into a golden shade, with John as the top figure.

This was the strange encounter of John and the forgotten shade. The last words of the shade to John were "I've got you at last, you fool."

The Sword and the Jade

Myth is a word which has, so to speak, come down in the world. Today, if we say that a statement is a myth, we mean that it is false and unworthy to be believed by intelligent people. Hence, many people are unwilling to admit that there are myths and legends, for instance in the time of the Greek civilization, many mythologies were set in the time of the ancients. The ancients being the gods, the Gorgons, and the giants, these all came into existence since man the mortal was not ready to rule. When these gods took over, the earth and the heavens became enraged in wars and strange powers – these powers were hell-sent.

This is the start of one such story, the myth of the sword and the jade. We start in the present, the year was 1948, a cargo ship comes into the port's dock for repair and provisions, also not forgetting the secret documents. These had been stored away in the Egyptian museum, for safe keeping to stop them from deteriorating and from being misused in any evil deeds. These documents had travelled a long way, half-way round the world, before being entombed in the Egyptian museum, then a day later, two official gentlemen from the ministry had arrived from London, commissioned by the British government to transfer the documents to a hidden location. This location was only known to the two officials, Dr Samuals and Mr Harding, as we rejoin them coming off the ship, walking down the gangplank.

Then as they were just going to step on to Greek territory, they were accosted by a party of Greek officials. One of them was warning Dr Samuals and Mr Harding not to tamper with the unknown, then Dr Samuals confronted the man and said, "Go away, you silly man."

One of the other officials said "If you want guides don't go in the city, as this myth is taboo."

15

So Dr Samuals and Mr Harding set off for a little town outside the city to look for a guide. This took them all afternoon, then when they reached the tiny town it was nearly dark. So the two of them set up their tents outside the town in a little field, then as they were snuggling up in their sleeping bags, Dr Samuals heard something. As he turned to Mr Harding to wake him up the noise had stopped. Mr Harding said, "What do you want?"

Dr Samuals replied, "Didn't you hear that noise?"

Mr Harding said, "What noise? Must have been the wind you heard."

"No it wasn't the wind."

Mr Harding said "Go back to sleep for God's sake, we have a big day tomorrow."

The next morning, Dr Samuals and Mr Harding were up at the crack of dawn, to look for their guide in the town. While they were looking around in the town they saw a "for sale' sign up on one of the town's streets, so they knocked on the door, and asked for the guide. When he came out, Dr Samuals and Mr Harding signed him up on the spot for the long journey ahead. Not knowing what evils lay in wait for them, all three set off for the Sinah, with all their provisions. As they got twenty-five miles out of the town, they came across an old well, which had dried up due to the heat, so Dr Samuals sat down on the brick well to look at his secret map. Then as he broke the seal, a huge gust of wind came out from nowhere and blew him off the wall. Mr Harding went to pick him up from the ground. When he did so, a voice came from nowhere and said, "Who are you to awaken the gods of the heavens?"

When Dr Samuals heard this he couldn't believe it. Where was it coming from? As he looked round he could not see anything. Then as Mr Harding picked up Dr Samuals fully, the wind which had blown him had ceased, but in its place was the start of a sandstorm. So Dr Samuals bent down to pick up the map from the sand. As he did so, something weird happened to them and the map. They were transported through the unknown, and beyond the mysteries of time. Their journey was taking them through the Greek cosmos, either side of them were pictures of Greek heroes, such as Hercules who defied the gods, as well as Perseus, another son of Zeus who was sent out to fetch the head of Medusa. All this was flashing by,

16

plus Pluto who gave Perseus the helmet which made him invisible. On his way back from his many conquests he found a maiden called Andromeda chained to the rock of the sea, and after freeing her they married.

Theseus the Athenian delivered his country from the fearful yearly tribute to Crete of seven youths and seven maidens who were to be sacrificed to the Gorgon monster. This was accompanied by Jason and the Argonauts, who went in search of the Golden Fleece.

As they came to the end of their journey, through the Greek hall of fame, they drifted down to a sandy beach. While Dr Samuals and Mr Harding went for a walk on the beach, they looked round and saw their guide still with his eyes closed and shaking with fear. Mr Harding started to laugh, and when the guide heard this he opened his eyes, as he did so he saw that he was on the sandy beach. He began to panic, and Dr Samuals quickly ran over to him to calm him down.

Even Dr Samuals and Mr Harding were puzzled about what had happened, but they did not want to show it to the guide. Then as they were walking with the guide along the beach, Mr Harding realized the map had gone. The Doctor said to Mr Harding, "Where did you have it last?"

"It was in my hand, when we went through the time tunnel of Greek fame."

"You must have mislaid it in the time tunnel."

Mr Harding shouted "No, don't say we came all this way for nothing, then losing it at the last."

Then as the three of them sat down in disgust, the sand beneath them started to vibrate and as they looked up they saw the most horrifying sight of all. A Titan in full armour, it was looking at them from a distance, his expression was terrifying. They ran for their lives. The Titan started after them, his stride was fifty times larger than theirs, so he covered more ground. When Dr Samuals looked back, he saw the Titan gaining ground on them, so he shouted to the other two to separate. The guide in panic jumped into the sea and started to swim. When the Titan glanced over he saw the lone figure in the sea swimming about, then he glanced back to the other two, wondering which ones to go after. In a split second, he pounced on the lone swimmer in the sea as he put his hand down to scoop up the guide. A mighty roar was heard out to sea, when

17

the Titan stopped and glanced up he saw a huge dust cloud forming and increasing in speed.

The guide started to swim away from the Titan, who at this stage was too busy looking at the dust cloud. When the guide got to shore, he ran for his life to a secluded cave which was near the place where he first jumped from the Titan. When he got inside, Dr Samuals and Mr Harding were already there. The guide was taken aback, because he thought that they had run another way. When Dr Samuals saw the expression on the guide's face, he knew that he was puzzled. So he started to explain, while Mr Harding took a look outside to see what was happening. As he did so, a huge gust of wind sped past at a colossal speed.

Mr Harding was knocked back into the cave. Dr Samuals said, "What happened to you?"

Mr Harding replied, "Have a look outside, I think the dust cloud has arrived."

As he glanced outside, he saw the greatest sight of all, a Titan fighting the dust cloud which was encircling him. While the Titan was trying to fend off the advances of the dust cloud, it was slowly choking him to death. The Titan snorted his last breath, then took one last swipe at the cloud and keeled over, crashing down into the sea. The force as he hit was equivalent to a tidal wave. As the waves began to grow, Dr Samuals said "Oh my God."

Mr Harding heard this and came rushing over to the entrance to the cave. The waves were fifty feet in height, and increasing with every second. When they saw this coming at them, all three started running down the cave. When they reached halfway, Dr Samuals looked back at the entrance of the cave. At that precise moment, a mighty bang was felt, the tidal wave hit the entrance with such force that it was felt through the rock structures of the cave.

The water gushed by, all three were swept under. While they were drifting in and out of consciousness, the wave was taking them down into the deep holes of the unknown. Then as they bobbed up and down in the wave, the wave was decreasing in speed, then a couple of seconds later it had come to a complete stop. As the three of them were drifting on the surface still numbed at the effect of the tidal wave, their limbs were still shaking. Then as they drifted over, the wave had brought them to a secluded labyrinth underground, and Dr Samuals started to come out of his dazed state.

He was astounded to see where the wave had brought them, then as he glanced around at his colleagues he saw them floating on top of the water. So he went over to them, and slowly pulled them to the side of the cave where there was an embankment. While they were recuperating on the embankment, Dr Samuals went for a look around in the labyrinth. Twenty feet along the embankment, he stumbled on five open tunnels, which had warnings over four of them but the fifth one was left empty. Dr Samuals said to himself, "What could this mean? Is the fifth tunnel good, or evil as hell?"

When the other two fully recovered they glanced around them imagining that they should have been dead. They noticed Dr Samuals looking at the five tunnels. When the guide and Mr Harding met up with Dr Samuals, he was still bemused by these tunnels. Mr Harding said, "What shall we do?"

Dr Samuals did not know what to say. The guide was getting frightened.

So while the other two were making up their minds about which tunnel to go down, the guide slipped down one of the tunnels which had the warning sign. The other two looked round, to see where he had gone. Mr Harding said, "Where is the guide?"

Dr Samuals replied, "I don't know, shall I go and look for him? If he went down one of the warning tunnels he could be in danger."

Mr Harding said, "We could get lost if we go looking for him."

So Dr Samuals and Mr Harding refrained from entering the tunnel, and set off back to the labyrinth to set up camp. When they were building their camp, a terrifying screech was heard from one of the tunnels. As they glanced over to where the noise was coming from, a mauve and blue glow was seen. It had a pulsating hum, which was causing the whole labyrinth to vibrate and shudder. As Dr Samuals felt and heard this horrible sound, he felt himself being drained. Mr Harding became another victim to the humming sound, as both of them fell to the floor in agony with their hands over their ears for protection.

A couple of seconds later, the humming sound had ceased, and they got to their feet and took their hands down from their ears. Dr Samuals went over to the tunnel where the screech had come from, and as he did so the guide stumbled out of the tunnel with a look of horror on his face. Dr Samuals rushed over to him, in a frantic attempt to stop him from hitting the ground. But it was all in vain because the guide passed out and smashed on to the ground with a thump. As the doctor and Mr Harding saw this, their first reaction was to hurry to his aid. Then their next thought was that he was dead. They saw some horrific marks on his back, cauterized and burnt with such force. Then as they were inspecting the body, something inside it was reacting with their body heat, it was changing all its dimensions and molecules.

When they saw this transition, they stepped back in shock, they saw the body just disintegrate in front of their eyes. Suddenly the body emerged again, then vanished without any trace into the realms of the unknown, all-seeing and all-knowing. The mark where the body was had left a strange indentation in the ground. It looked like a sword and a jade, encircled by a Gorgon with a fire breath, and the Gorgon had a Satan image imprinted on its back. Then as Dr Samuals and Mr Harding went for a closer look, the image was slowly fading, but as they tried to save it from going, a terrifying cry was heard. As they looked up, they saw the most horrific sight, it was a Gorgon with the head of a scorpion and a cow's back and legs.

They ran for cover. The Gorgon trotted after them with his scorpion's head lashing out at every opportunity. As the Doctor and Mr Harding were running they caught sight of a hole in the cave's wall, so they stopped running and climbed into it, as fast as they could go. Dr Samuals got in quickly, but Mr Harding was caught halfway through the hole, as the Doctor was pushing and pulling him. The Gorgon was on the verge of catching Mr Harding when the Doctor pulled at the last moment. Then when the Gorgon snapped away at the hole, he found it empty.

The Gorgon went away in disgust, sissing and hissing as it found no meal for itself. Dr Samuals said, "That was too close for comfort."

"Close is not the word."

Then as both of them looked, they found that the hole they had come through was shrinking in size. When Dr Samuals saw this, he shouted at Mr Harding to stop it, as he tried with all his might to stop the decreasing phenomenon, but as he tried again it seemed to stop for a second. But it was all in vain, because the next second it started again and this time the hole went, sealing itself with its rock magma.

They were entombed. Dr Samuals said, "This is another fine mess you have got me into Mr Harding, my faithful friend."

"It wasn't my fault the Gorgon came after us, was it?"

"I suppose not, all things considered."

As they waited in the rocks, the days came and went, by this time the temperature inside the rocks was increasing with every second. Then suddenly a tremor was felt, then all of a sudden it stopped, then it started again, this time with a horrific jolt which made the rocks above them fall. Dr Samuals and Mr Harding put their arms up to stop the falling debris from hurting them.

Then when a couple of seconds went by, the tremor had ceased, leaving a dust cloud inside the rock cabin. While the dust was settling, they had been engulfed in dust as they lifted all the rocks off themselves. They glanced up to the ceiling and saw daylight. When they saw this the both of them went berserk with delight, but when they had calmed down from this excitement, Dr Samuals said "How do we get up there?"

Mr Harding replied, "With great difficulty."

Then Dr Samuals had a brainstorm. "This is what we shall do, my old friend."

He bent down and said to Mr Harding, "Get on my back and lift yourself up into the hole where the daylight is coming from."

As Mr Harding did this, he pulled himself up with all his might. When he got through the hole, he noticed that it was an old corridor of wooden piles untouched for thousands of years. He was so spellbound that he forgot about his friend, who at this time was shouting for all his worth. Then Mr Harding came out of the trance, and shook his head from left to right to get back his senses. After he had done this he strutted over to where the Doctor was. When he reached the hole he heard the doctor shouting up, "Are you there?"

Then the Doctor said, "Where have you been all this time?"

21

"I got carried away, sorry."

"Help me up."

Mr Harding put his hand down through the hole. The Doctor put his arm up but could not reach. He noticed a large rock on the ground next to him, so he dragged it along the ground, and positioned the rock underneath the hole, and slowly stood on it. Then as the Doctor put his arm up again Mr Harding grabbed it and started to pull him up, then as the Doctor was fully through the hole he was also spellbound by the preserved wood and rock formation. He came out of his trance, and shaking his head from left to right, his thoughts went back to the rock, which he had stood on to get up from the rock cabin. Dr Samuals said, "But I didn't notice that there before."

"Maybe you missed it the first time round."

"I'm sure I didn't."

While they were walking, they got twenty feet down the preserved fossilized corridor, when they came across a stone wedged in the sand. They couldn't believe their eyes, then as Mr Harding got close to it, the stone started to sink. Then as it submerged from view, they heard this almighty bang, and both of them ducked down in panic, to avoid any debris flying by. Then as Dr Samuals looked up and Mr Harding turned around, all they saw was a misty dust cloud obstructing their view. Then as they stared the mist was settling around them, they could just see a white figure standing upright. Dr Samuals could see a white robed man, and alongside him was a unicorn. Mr Harding was amazed and said, "It can't be."

Dr Samuals said, "It is, it's Pegasus, but this is impossible because it died out a long time ago."

Then the old man spoke, he said, "Do you seek the sword and the jade?"

Dr Samuals said "Yes", then the old man said, "Then follow the unicorn down the corridor of the gods."

So both of them followed the unicorn, to its unknown destination and beyond, down the corridor they went, watching and admiring the form of the unicorn. They went another thirty feet down the corridor, when suddenly they came across a very old gate which had two drums of water hanging on it. Then the unicorn gave a roar and vanished through the gate of the unknown.

Then the old door spoke, saying, "So you seek the sword and the jade, then as a test, which of these is water in my drums?"

When the doctor heard this, he said, "That's easy", then in an instant Mr Harding stopped him from saying one more word. The Doctor said "What's the matter?"

Mr Harding said, "It could be a trick to coax us in." Then he shouted out, "No water is here."

Then when the door heard this, it became unbalanced and started to vibrate, as it did so a huge boulder was let loose, it was heading straight for them from behind. Both of them leaned back on the door with fear, and with their arms crossed in front of their eyes to shield them from the impending doom. Then, as they were pinned down, it all went quiet and they opened their eyes to find a giant steel door had come across the corridor. It had cut the boulder in two, they could not believe it, it was heading straight for them. Then as they turned around, the door was bellowing smoke, then a bang was heard, the blast was so strong it blew them into the unknown. When they came to, they were in Egypt in the year 1952, Dr Samuals and Mr Harding had been transported through time. But where were the sword and the jade, were they lost forever?

This was our story. Who knows where it lies?

Possession

Possession. This is a word which many people use without knowing definitely what they mean by it. It's possession of the soul, they say. In days gone by evil done was penalized by torment of the living soul, and the fellowship of hell. When this came to pass, the possessed had a feeling of union with the self, creating a craven image of the self in the face of Satan. They thought that they were the only objects in the whole universe, and tended to see God as the evil one, when all in all God was the purified one.

Now the story you are going to hear about happened on October 31, Halloween night. Frank Thomas, a well-known engineer was getting into his car. When he started to drive off, he found that his car would not start, so he got out to have a look underneath the bonnet. The bonnet was stuck, then suddenly something came up behind him, and said "trick or treat", so Frank being the friendliest of people said, "O.K., treat", then as he turned his back to get his fingers out from beneath the bonnet's locking system, he looked round again and found that the person had gone.

When he looked round and down the street, even in the undergrowth and through the hedges he found nothing, the person or thing had vanished off the face of the earth. His face said it all, he was baffled beyond belief. Frank said to himself, "How could he have moved so fast, even without leaving a trace of some kind?" Then as he shook his head from side to side in puzzlement, he slowly got into his car, and this time when he started his ignition his car started first time, without any trouble or stalling even. He was amazed and stunned.

Then Frank said, "What was the matter with you, had you been possessed?" As he stárted driving down his drive-way, and on to the street, he had to stop again, only this time it was party revellers strolling across the roadway. Fifty yards down the street, he noticed something in his rear mirror, then as he glanced up again the thing had gone. Frank said to himself, "This is uncanny." So he carried on driving down the street, as he did so a strong wind whipped up, lashing against his car, causing his steering wheel to veer to the left.

Then as he tried to straighten up, his car locks went down in the locking position, when Frank heard this he tried with all his might with one hand on the steering wheel to get back his doors to their normal position, as he took off down the street with a frantic look on his face. He started talking to himself, saying "What do you want with me?" His eyes wandered from the road for one second, and as he glanced back a boy was standing in the road. Frank shouted to him to get out of the way, then Frank put his hands up to his face in panic as he took his hands off the steering wheel. The car veered into a tree, and Frank was thrown through his windscreen, and on to the ground.

At this stage, Frank was lying helpless on the ground, then as he opened his eyes blood was everywhere, his eyes were glazed over with his blood. As he flicked his eyelids, he noticed a black figure coming towards him, but as he tried to move, all his arms and legs were paralyzed and painful with the movement. Then the figure spoke, saying, "You are mine now, so say goodbye to this world Frank Thomas."

"How do you know my name?"

"I am Lucifer the hell devil, now do you know me"

Frank said, "Oh my God," then the figure said, "Who is your god?"

Frank shouted at the figure, "More powerful than you will ever be."

"No one is stronger than the almighty Lucifer, only I am the powerful one." Frank then said, "You are nothing compared to God."

Then the devil let out a mighty roar of disapproval, and said in an echo, "Who is this god you dare to speak of?"

"He is the all-powerful one."

Then as Frank spoke these words, the devil spun round faster than Frank could blink. "So can your god do that?"

Frank replied, "My God can do that twice as fast."

Then the devil said, "I have had enough of this, repent now because in a second you are going to be in hell, this is my birth place, you will feel at home there."

Frank said, "No, I won't, because this is my home."

Lucifer stood there gazing into Frank's eyes. Then he said, "Open your mouth, because I want your soul."

Frank tried with all his might to withstand his power, but it was too strong.

Then as he lay there in fear of his life, the devil expelled all the air in his lungs and blew it into Frank's body. As Frank felt this happening he tried resisting again but it was no good. The devil said to him, "Be brave and all will be well."

The force that was going inside him was pure evil. Frank's last words were, "Help me God, I plead with you." Then the force began to have its effect on Frank, as he came to he could not feel any pain. As he started to walk up the street his legs and arms were dripping blood all over the place, and when he saw this he just laughed. As he spoke his face was disjointed and out of sequence. As he went fifty yards down the street, he came across a boy playing trick or treat, so he asked the boy to come over. When the boy looked up, his face was frightened, terrified to go up to strangers.

Then as the remains of Frank's body, with the evil force inside him, went up to the boy, the boy saw this and took off down the street, screaming and shouting as he went. When the boy reached the bottom of the street, he came across a group of policemen standing outside talking to each other. When the boy saw these he rushed up to them, as he did so one of the policemen turned round and said, "What do you want, boy"

The boy stood with his mouth open but no words coming out. Then the policeman turned to his fellow officers, and said, "Here boys, we have a scared kid here, be quiet a minute. Tell us what's upsetting you, and you lot be quiet, the boy is trying to tell us something important. Go on boy, I'm all ears."

Then as the boy spoke, the policeman noticed a strange figure standing at the end of the street, then the boy saw him glancing down the street. He pushed past the policeman for a better look, as he did so he saw the sight that he didn't want to see, the devil. The boy fainted and the policeman rushed over to see how he was. When he got there, he found that the boy had turned white in colour, then he knelt down in front of the boy. The policeman picked up his head from the ground, the boy opened his eyes and looked straight up at him and said, "Lucifer is here." When the policeman heard this, he looked at his colleagues and nodded to them.

Then he looked back at the boy, the boy's eyes were green in colour. The policeman said, "Oh my God", then the boy said, "But there is no God."

Then he gave an echoed shout, and said, "I am here, this is my possession, for this is my hell and all eternity and for evermore." Then he looked into the policeman's eyes and said "I live", then vanished without a trace.

Arizona Experiment

During the 1950s, Arizona and other regions of the United States of America were test stations for the ministry of defence. Their uses were varied and different such as nuclear to biological warfare. One such station was commissioned for that specific purpose. It was called the Arizona Experiment, this project was in the first Arizona Bunker.

The scientist in charge on this fateful day was Sam Hollis. Sam's work was involved with the destruction of living matter. One day, Sam was delivering a barrel of living matter to the processing plant. While he was waiting for the lift, he put the barrel down on the floor for a little rest. What he did not realize was that he had put it down right next to a doorway, and unbeknown to Sam a porter was coming up at that exact moment. When the porter opened the door, the lift arrived as all the people were getting out, all pushing and barging. The barrel was upset and fell over, and started to leak all around the corridor. Alarm bells started to ring around the building, Sam was getting frightened.

"It's leaking," the porter cried, "Oh my God, I can't breathe."

When Sam saw this he ran as fast as he could into the lift, and as he got in the whole barrel burst open. When the lift doors closed, Sam could see the matter turning a green colour, all he could hear was screaming.

When the lift arrived at the basement, he got out and started to run up the corridor for all his worth. Then suddenly he heard a strange noise, it was coming from the lift vent. It had got to the cables. When Sam heard this he did not look back, then as he got to the main crossroads he did not know which way to go. Then he heard a howl of evil, he ran down the closest corridor, where he met a colleague. As they got to the door where the germ was, as they looked in, they saw the remains of Sam's colleague. When the boss saw this he could not believe his eyes. He shouted to Sam, "Go up to my office, and phone for help."

While Sam was doing this, his boss was still looking into the lab, and then all of a sudden, the germ came towards the window. When the boss saw this, he edged backwards with fear. Sam was just phoning when he heard this deafening shout of fear. When he put the phone down, he ran down to see what the shouting was. When he got halfway there he saw the germ on his boss, it had shattered the glass window of the lab. While Sam was watching, the germ sensed this, and started after him.

He started running for his life. When he looked back, he saw the germ coming towards him, when he saw this he ran through the nearest door he could find. When he got into the room he slammed it shut behind him, as it was shut he was looking around the room for some seal to clog-up the door with. When he found something, the germ was outside trying to get into the room. While Sam was plugging the door up with the seal, as he looked out of the peep-hole on the door, he noticed that the germ was nowhere to be seen. He started to worry and became frantic.

When Sam calmed down, he noticed on the other side of the room a ventilation grill, and he went over to have a look. He started to unscrew the loose screws that were holding up the grill, and got the four screws out and lifted the grill. He could see that the ventilation was clear, so he got inside, and started to crawl along the ventilation unit. When he got 500 feet into the unit, Sam sensed something was wrong up ahead.

When he got closer, as he came up to it, he could see that the noise was an air re-cooling system. The system was inside a lighted room, as Sam saw this he started to climb down. When he eventually got down, he could see that the room was an old warehouse. When he got 300 feet along the warehouse, he could see an old door, and he tried to open it. When he did so, the door seemed to creak open with age. When he eventually got the door open, he could see a road, so he started to run out into the road. When he got 300 yards up the road, he looked up and saw the germ above him. He said, "Oh my God", then as he was running, the germ hit him, and started to engulf him in a cloud. This was the story of Sam Hollis.

The Sun Probe

The year was 1995, NASA had launched her first sun probe. NASA wanted to harness the sun's power, the sun probe was an expedition, to find out if the sun's power could be harnessed and confined. The two astronauts involved were Dr David Benton and Charley Hawk. This was their mission, and their story of the sun probe.

Day One. The sun probe orbits round the moon, to shield against the sun's rays. Halts its position, Charley comes on mike, saying "What's our position?". NASA replies, "Moon orbit twenty-five miles southwest of sun."

Day Two. David Benton accelerates the sun probe's boosters. As he did so, one of them misfired, and faded. He tried it again, still no use, then as he looked at the rear panel, he could see that the optical stage was not catching. When David Benton saw this, his nerves got the better of him. He started to panic. When Charlie saw this his mood changed, he said to David, "If the booster won't catch, we will have to rig something else up."

But David said, "We will drift into the sun's gravity."

Charley with his nerves of steel, underneath was shaking like a leaf.

Day Three. Charles Hawk improves oxygen output, tried rear booster again, still no good.

Day Four. Still drifting in towards the sun's gravity, trying the probe's boosters again, fires but not enough going to rely on one booster.

Day Five. Charles' mood comes and goes. Tried the operational unit, to rest all the systems. Then as David was sorting out the system analyzer, he noticed out of the rear window an asteroid belt. While they were travelling through, one of the asteroids hit the surplus engine. It caused a course deflection. Charley said "What's wrong?"

David said, "I don't know if we are heading for the sun still, because the hit has caused the gyro to malfunction. We could be heading out to open space."

Charles replied, "Can't we alter the amount of carbon dioxide that goes in the relay tank?"

David said, "No, because the amount is negligible, and also the relay tank has lost half its oxygen."

Charles was deliberating what to do next. He said to David, "One of us has to go outside."

"Which one out of the two of us?" David replied. "The one with the most experience stays inside," David said, "that's me."

So Charles went to the suit chamber. As he was suiting up, David was checking that the way was clear outside. When Charles was ready, he flicked up the button on the locking door, and as he did so, a supernova had occurred on the sun. Its force was intense and penetrating, as Charles was just outside the door. A huge space shock-wave was felt, as it came overhead, its pressurized force took Charles into the path of the sun.

When Charles went past the ship, David at this time was still checking out the boosters. When he looked out of the window for just a moment, he saw his colleague floating towards the sun. When he saw this, David floated down the corridor as fast as he could, to the suit chamber. Then as he got his space-helmet on, the radio inside his helmet came on. Charles was calling, saying, "Forget about me, save yourself, end of message."

Then there was quite a deafening silence, as Charles went into the sun's mouth. After hearing this David was in a paralyzed state, and shell-shocked. His friend had gone from his midst, now the mission was up to him. There were fifteen minutes until impact with the sun's orbit and gravitational pull. So David got to work straight away, to see what he could do about the boosters. While he was looking at the decapsulate mode, the asteroid belt had moved into the sun's orbit. The sun was still intensifying in heat, and its atmosphere was increasing in size. Its force was pulling all the asteroids into its inner core.

Day Six. Within five minutes the ship will be no more, David at this stage was writing his last log. When he looked out of the window, he saw the full horror of the sun beaming down on him. So he said, "Goodbye world", as the ship slowly sank into the flames of hell.

This was the story of sun probe station log 15, by David Benton.

Materialization

This story is the result of a long and deep search. A search is like a question and as such provides no clue to the relationship of the searcher to the object of this deep search. The person who asks must not necessarily believe whatever is out there, but he longs for an explanation. The inquiring mind looks for a confirmation or a negation, eventually an answer will be found to these searching questions.

The start of this story was in 1890, the year when scientific aspirations were to the fore. When different countries were competing for the ultimate prize, the prize of a new discovery. This is the story of one of those discoveries, when patience had to be a virtue, the professor in question was Samual Porter. His works included the transmission of light reflecting off the planets, and its wave ratio.

While he was working one stormy night, inside his little lab, he was trying to focus in on Jupiter's moon when a strange thing happened. While he was focussing, something out of the ordinary was happening. A materialization of some sort, as he focused properly he could see it. He was astounded, it was the face of Kronos the fallen god. He couldn't take his eyes off it, then as he was looking through his telescope, still looking at the figure, he became unbalanced on his stool with fright. When he fell on to the floor below him, he upset his telescope which began to spin in a circular motion. While it was spinning, a figure began to appear in a black and white negative image. While he was watching this, a voice began to speak. "Who are you to disturb my peace?" As it was talking, the professor slowly reached for his metal rod, to try and counter its electrical field, which was like a thread of pure energy.

As Samuel slowly got up, the figure started to move towards him, right up to his face. The figure tried to bond with Samual's body, as it did so, the metal bar which the professor

33

was holding counteracted with the electrical figure. When the figure felt this, it was thrown back with such force that it ended up on the other side of the lab.

While the professor was recovering, the metal rod which he was holding at the time of impact fell to the ground, The rod had turned a strange mauve colour, and it was glowing with a pulsating noise ringing out from it. When the figure had recovered from its jolt, it started to move towards the professor. When the professor saw this he began to get frightened, because his only source of protection was half way across the room.

When the figure saw this metal bar lying across the room, glowing, his face began to change. While the figure was busy looking at the metal bar, the professor saw a weird thing. The bar was changing. Its whole structure was changing, and its colour was illuminating, and as the figure moved closer to the bar, it began to exude a gluey substance. This strange thing was moving towards the figure, as it did so it was like a spiral cord twisting and turning. When the gluey substance finally got to the figure, the cord which was twisting and turning stopped dead in its tracks. When the figure saw this it began to get nervous and started slowly walking back. The cord, which was lying dormant, started to twirl round and round like a spinning top. When it finally came to a standstill, the professor was looking on with an intriguing thought. Was this the forces of good and evil?

Then as the professor was still looking, the gluey substance's front opened up, out came a man. When the professor looked closer, the man reminded him of something. He said, "Of course, Thor the god of war. If these two fight it out, who knows what destruction will be done."

While Thor was looking at the figure of the fallen god, his eyes illuminated with a thick red brightness. Then it let loose this almighty shot of laser light, which pierced the figure's outer seal which was the fallen god's only protection. When this light hit, it began to set off a chain-reaction.

The pressure of this made him faint, as he fainted the ceiling above the two figures opened up. A huge whirl-wind began to suck up everything in sight, and a couple of seconds later, the professor began to regain his senses. When he opened his eyes, the whirl-wind began to suck him into its inner core, as the

34

professor felt this he began to grab on to anything handy. When the wind hit full strength, the professor was thrown across the room, and all his instruments flew into the core like a magnetic overflow. Confronted by his impending death, he prayed, and as he closed his eyes he began to feel the wind decrease.

When he opened his eyes, he saw a glazed mirror in front of him as he let go of the bar he was holding. He gradually ventured over to it with a guided apprehension, but he was intrigued by this mirror. When he got up close to it, a strange feeling came over him as though somebody was watching him from the other side. Then as he turned his head round for a moment's thought, a huge hand came out of the mirror.

As he saw this the professor did not have a chance the hand was too strong, it pulled him into the other side of hell. While he was being transported through the depths of space, he could see vast galaxies, and stars glittering with brightness, and the hand began to accelerate with speed. When he began to feel the gravity pull, his whole body began to wither and deteriorate under the extreme pressures.

As the hand was moving through the time boundaries, he began to realize he was ageing with an accelerated pace. When the professor looked down at his hands all his skin was peeling. The huge hand had come to a standstill. In front of them was a white room with white furniture, the hand opened his grasp on the professor to let him down. When it did so the professor was slowly drifting down through the galaxies, until finally he came to rest on the white room's floor. As he began to stand up, he suddenly glanced over to the mirror which was opposite him. When he did he found to his horror that the mirror contained another solar system, as his eyes penetrated deep down into its subconscious he could see its organic entity. The professor said, "Was this its interstellar ex-void, the sun, the planets, and satellites?"

The activity he was looking at was the reverse of our solar system, the heliocentric positions of the planets had resigned to a negative influence. When the professor glanced away from the mirror, the mirror began to change and its whole structure was altering. He stepped back in amazement, then out of nowhere a huge fire ball burst through the mirror, at the same moment a blue brightness fell on to the whole room. When the blue brightness came to a stop, it engulfed the professor, sealing him for eternity. It also created a vacuum which extinguished the fire ball, as the professor was witnessing this his whole body began to deteriorate. Then suddenly his legs gave way underneath him, as he was resting on the floor.

He started to think back years again to the start of the discovery. While he was doing this, a form of gas smoke was excreted into the blue field that was keeping the professor. When the smoke engulfed the whole field, the professor was made immobile as the transference was proceeding. A voice was heard. "This is Thor. This is the only solution, sorry professor."

Then as the professor came to, he found himself back on his labs stool and everything was back to normal. Or was it?

This is the story of professor Samuel 1895.

The Wreck

The place was Naples, the year was 1863. A ship had just anchored near the shore, a three-mast cutty sark. It had stopped for provisions, for its next mission or encounter. The captain of this ship was an old Dartmouth man, upright and coarse, his crew were made up from a mixed bunch of rascals and drunks.

Before the ship could set sail for its next mission, its rigging had to be checked for fatigue. This was either supervised by the captain, or his second-in-command, which in this case was a new boy called Sach. Now Sach was one of these greenhorns just passed out of Dartmouth College, as an officer and a gentleman. So for his first day aboard ship, his first duty of the day was to break in the new crew. While he was getting up the courage to do this, the captain was keeping a careful eye on him. While Sach was talking to the crew, the captain sensed that the crew was getting agitated, with his lack of knowledge aboard ship. Then as the captain saw the impending danger down below on the deck, he shouted down to them, "All hands set sail."

When this command was heard, all the crew got down to work. The anchor was pulled in, and was secured tight around a metal pilon, next the sails were checked to see that there were no flaws or gashes. Then as the ship was passing the sea-wall barrier, the whole crew was so engrossed in their work, that they had forgotten about Sach. While the crew were engrossed in their work, Sach stood alongside one of the masts and looked out to sea. By this time the ship was slowly threading its way through the waves.

As the days and months passed, still no sign of land in any direction. The wind at this time had ceased, making the ship stagnate in the sea as the days wore on with still no change in the weather. There was no wind to be felt anywhere, the crew were getting bored and irritable, and also the rations were getting low. The captain could sense something was wrong, and as he was on the verge of shouting at the crew, an almighty clash of thunder was heard from above. The captain was taken back with shock, then as he looked out to sea he saw a menacing black cloud forming, it was gaining strength from the whirl-pool which was forming underneath it. Then all of a sudden a thick grey sludge was unleashed from its jaws, on to the ship's port and aft. When the captain saw what was happening he called down to the crew to abandon ship, and the crew shouted up towards the bridge "Captain, the sludge is moving in towards the ship!"

The captain did not say anything, but just stood there admiring this strange phenomenon. By this time the sludge was creeping up the masts and down the cabins, when Sach saw this happening he ran up the nearest stairs. The captain was looking out to sea, still bemused and with a disturbed expression on his face, as Sach got up to the captain he found him paralyzed and shaking with fear. Sach shouted at him, "Captain, get off the ship!"

As he got no answer, Sach started to shake him, then he slapped his face. When the captain looked round, he started to laugh, with this Sach walked back in disbelief. Sach was saying to himself, "What shall I do? I can't leave him."

Then out of nowhere, a huge bolt of lightning hit the sea below them, it had caused a chain-reaction, everything around them started to spit with static. While this was happening up on the bridge, the crew were trying to fend off the sludge on the deck, while Sach went over to the captain, this time to force him to see reason. When he turned him round, Sach shouted with horror. The captain was just a skeleton, as Sach pushed it aside.

The captain just disintegrated in front of him. When Sach saw this he took fright, as he was running to dive off the ship, to his horror he found himself in slow-motion. When he started to shout, his voice came out all garbled, when he got to the port barrier to dive off, as he was getting ready to dive, a piercing white light was thrown down on to the ship. It stunned Sach for a few moments, as his eyes were caught unawares, he became disorientated and unbalanced. The next moment he felt himself falling over the side, towards the sea. As he was just going to touch the sea, he was stuck in mid-air.

When this happened, Sach tried to break free but it was no good, the intense pressure was too much. Sach looked over his shoulder to see if he could see the rest of the crew. The sludge was eating away parts of the ship, and the crew were nowhere to be seen. Sach could not look any more, the brightness was too much. As he closed his eyes for a moment's lapse, he felt himself being carried away.

When he opened his eyes again all he felt was the waves crashing against his face, and his hands had gripped an old piece of wood which was floating next to him. When he looked up to see where the ship was, and where he was, he caught sight of a shiny object in the distance. When Sach started to swim over to it, he found to his amazement that he could not move his legs. The sea at this time was becoming choppy, it started to knock him from side to side. The ferocious sea began to increase in strength, by this time Sach was trying to swim with the aid of his piece of wood and getting quite frantic. He was just coping with this awkward way of swimming, when out of the blue he caught sight of the ship, it was still intact.

To his joy the ship was drifting towards him, and he began to increase his strokes. The ship at this time was cutting through the waves, Sach was going up and down like a yoyo in the sea. A couple of minutes later, the ship drew up alongside him, and with all his might he grabbed the ropes which were dangling in the sea. Then as the ship took off again Sach was holding on for dear life, the waves were crashing against the sides of the ship making big gaping holes. While Sach was climbing up, he found to his amazement that his legs were back to normal. When he reached the deck he found it empty, it was like a ghost ship as he was walking towards the ship's cabin. On the deck was a white mist, every time he walked on it it seemed to make a noise.

Suddenly there was a loud crack in the sky, and as he looked up Sach saw fiery rocks hurtling down towards the ship. These rocks of fire were so intense that they turned the sky red. Sach's eyes were glued to these funny objects. It was as though he were witnessing a new beginning as they came accelerating down. Sach jumped. When he landed in the sea the rocks hit the ship with venom, as Sach came to the surface all he saw was a wreck of a ship. Then as he started to swim over to it, he could see on the other side of the ship a glowing green mist, which was increasing in size. As he got closer to it he could feel a ghostly presence, then as he was climbing up the ropes, Sach noticed a huge gash in the front end of the ship. The ship was slowly sinking. He saw a silvery figure standing near the archway of the cabin, near the deck. As Sach went over to see what it was, the figure started to walk down the stairs.

When Sach went to follow this strange figure, a deep voice echoed from the sky above him saying, "Stay where you are."

Sach said, "My name is SACH!"

The voice went quite silent. When Sach started to walk away, the green mist that was on the ship began to spin and spin and to his horror it started to creep towards him. When he started to back away from it, the voice said, "It's no good, you can't escape from it."

Sach tried going left and right, the same route as the mist went. Sach was cornered, as he was up against the wall.

Sach took a chance, and ran as fast as he could over the ship's side. Sach had made it, as he came up from the cold and forbidding sea he was alone, the ship was nowhere to be seen. Then as he looked over his shoulder, he could see land. He was delighted as he started to swim over to the island. While he was swimming he saw a cove. Sach said to himself, "Come on boy, just a few more miles and you're there. He swam and swam, until he finally made it. As he got into the cove, he could not believe it. The ship was anchored near the cove. "I thought you had gone, damn it," Sach said.

When he swam over to the shore, somebody was waiting for him. The man shouted out to him, "Are you okay?"

Sach said "Yes", as he started to walk over to him. The figure just vanished without a trace. As Sach started to walk across the beach, he walked about twenty yards when he was sucked into the depths of the unknown. He was accelerating downwards, with so much force that his face was being wrenched in all directions. Then as fast as it started, it stopped. He was stationary. Then suddenly a door opened in front of him. The lights which were coming out of it were terrific, all different colours. Sach said, "What is this infernal force?"

When he took a closer look, his hand passed through a force field. Suddenly he slipped down, he went into the realms of the nknown. His whole body was going around and around. A couple of moments later he found himself on a wreck. As he awoke properly, he was in a town's shore. He had been transported back to his original port of departure. Sach said a prayer for being alive. When Sach went on to the shore, an old man came up to him. "So you thought it was a dream?"

Sach said, "What? Oh my God, help me someone."

The Tower

In the beginning, cavemen prayed to the sky or objects abnormal in appearance, or objects which had that lasting impression. Be they cosmic, or supernatural visitors, these visitors would leave behind beacons, built to send messages to the future man. When hundreds of centuries had passed, these objects were still being worshipped by people of different religions, and different cultures. As the years moved on these beacons were covered with people's gifts and ornaments, of good intent or satanic fixtures. These fixtures when seen at night would glow, and when the people witnessed this strange happening on these beacons, they ceased to come anymore. Because of the sign of the devil being illuminated on these beacons, they became known as the beacons of the night.

These beacons were influenced by the sun at day, and the moon at night, influences which go back to the start of man's dawn. These cosmic influences became stronger as time went on, their power became dominant and forceful even upon the earth's magnetic field, having a disastrous effect by changing its magnitude. In order to understand this, man had to adapt to the principal variations and become more responsive to the change. Even though it was draining all the earth's power, these beacons had been strategically placed to capture the sun's flares, in order to become self-reliant. When the sun's heat touched the outer skin of the beacon, the heat caused the beacon to change appearance. This change was relative to a tower, this tower became known as a spirit of evil because of its resemblance to Satan's hell, and the mysterious unknown.

These towers were built as monuments, these were the time barriers to hell and the unknown cosmos. When the years rolled on they became submerged in marshland and buried and forgotten, until now. The year was 1890, the place was Hascon, near a little field off the beaten track lay the last

42

remnants of these mysterious towers. It had been preserved over millions of years, embedded in chalk and limestone and covered over with earth.

A scientist from the town of Hascon arrived at the place where the tower was buried. He ventured round the site, to see if any fossils were to be found hidden in the cracks around the tower's brick-work. While he was looking at the tower's brick-work, he felt the earth move underneath him. He noticed a hand come up from the ground where he was standing and start to write a couple of words in the ground beneath him. The words said "This is the Devil's Tower, keep away for your own safety." When John saw these being written with a dead hand, he fainted with fright.

When he came to after a couple of seconds on the ground, he awoke to find himself mysteriously covered with a strange algae. As he tried to take it off, its bondings became tighter around him. He did not know what to do for the best, whether to stand still or move about, while he was trying to make up his mind the algae just vanished without a trace. When John patted himself down to see that he was not dreaming, a voice came out from the tower saying, "I told you to leave."

Then John shouted out to the tower, "I will go when I am good and ready."

When John had finished saying this, a huge gust of wind made a bee-line for John. When he saw this coming towards him he tried to duck out of the way, but it was too late, the wind hit him dead-on with an enormous velocity. When the wind hit John, it made his hair stand on end and made his cheekbones sink into his face with abnormal pressure.

When the wind ceased, John was left standing in a paralyzed state of mind. When he fully recovered, he noticed that while he was in his state of motionlessness his position where he was standing had altered, and also the things around him had altered beyond all recognition. When his eyes glanced up he saw that the tower was not old anymore, it was almost brand new and covered with strange ornaments. These ornaments were shining so much they almost blinded John, as he turned his eyes away from the brightness.

As he turned his head round to focus on the tower again, he found to his horror a lone figure standing in the doorway. The figure was waving him in, and when John saw this he became frightened and was just on the verge of walking back as far as he could go. The figure put a tracking beam on John, when he felt this take hold of him he tried with all his might to break loose, but it was no good, the tracker beam was fixed. As the figure was pulling John towards itself, as John was unable to break loose he let the beam take him inside the tower. When the beam got to the doorway, along with John, it whisked him inside the tower then vanished without a trace, as John fell down with a thud on to the floor. He felt himself being taken for a journey into the unknown as he slowly stood up, and glanced around the inside as he did so. Everything around the tower was moving in sequence, as they were moving through time the brick-work was rotating round and round with such speed, that John became unbalanced. Suddenly they came to an abrupt end when the Tower stopped dead and the beams all stopped.

When this happened John went flying through the air, he was heading for the towers brick wall. When he noticed where he was heading, he quickly put his hands in front of his face, to stop himself from getting hurt. When he went flying into the wall, he went straight through it without a scratch and landed outside the tower. As he slowly took his hands away from his eyes, he noticed that he was inside a boggy marsh, and the figure that was inside the tower had emerged outside as well.

Then as he looked up at him, the figure glanced back at him in an unpleasant manner, and yet the menacing manner was tinged with a hidden meaning. When John went up to the figure, to confront him face-to-face, the figure shouted a high-pitched note, which was deafening to the ears of a human. When John put his hands up to his ears to muffle the noise, he saw the figure disappear in front of him. In its place was a golden chest. John stepped back in amazement, as he did so the chest started to open. The noise as the chest opened was quite deafening, when the chest fully opened, John uncovered his ears to hear nothing but silence. Then as he started to walk over to the chest, John became apprehensive because he did not know what he was going to find when he got there.

His eyes became fixed on a red, gluey substance which was gushing from the sides of the chest. When John got up close to this, he saw that the red gluey substance was printing something on the chest. When the substance had written on the chest, John peered over to look inside. A strange voice spoke, the dialect was nothing that he had ever heard, and then as he was listening a bolt of lightning came out of the chest. Its terrifying force caused a change in the gluey substance surrounding the chest. Its structure was demagnetizing the whole field around it. While John was watching this, his apprehension was growing by the minute, then suddenly John's fear was confirmed. In a split second, the chest exploded, throwing John into a state of paralyzed confusion.

John was transported into the black, unexplained outer space. He had witnessed the birth of a new star. When John looked at his hands he found to his amazement that the blast had affected his body dimensions. John could see right through himself, and he was floating through the outer regions of the solar system. He realized that he could breath in the vacuum, then as he glanced above, he saw what no other man has seen, a cluster of new-born stars. Then he realized he was in the Orion Nebula, his presence there seemed to create an unbalance in the Orion itself. The appearance of matter inside the Nebula was causing a change in the structural bonds, they were changing into V-particles and thus creating a bubble chamber. When John saw this happening in front of his eyes, he began to realize that he was caught in a matrix, then suddenly a burst of emissions from the adjoining matrix were travelling towards the Orion Nebula.

They were accelerating in speed, its mass was ten times greater than the Orion Nebula, by this time John was panicking and trying his hardest to break the bubble chamber which was sealing him in. While he was rummaging around in the bubble, the emissions were about fifty feet away and accelerating with every second. Then as John looked up he saw the emission heading straight for the place where he was, its appearance looked menacing and destructive. Then as a couple of seconds went by, the mass of emissions hit the Orion Nebula. The impact was so destructive that it fractured the bubble which was sealing him in. Then the fall-out blew John into outer space, with an accelerated speed that sent John into hyper-space. While he was spinning around and around in space, he felt himself suffocating with the lack of air, as he put his hands up to his throat, to try and contract some air bubbles.

Suddenly he passed out, as he was drifting through time and

dimensions. By this time his mind was in a subconscious state. While his mind was drifting, his outer self came to a complete stop. When he opened his eyes for a second he saw a bright white light coming towards him. Then everything went quiet around him, as he closed his eyes to make sure that he was not dreaming, and opened them again.

He found himself in a black chamber. As John fully awoke out of his state of lifeless motion, he slowly came to his feet and looked around him. He noticed that he was back in the tower, he had gone full circle. While he was looking round the tower's inner chamber, he noticed a white door which was half-open. When John started to walk towards it, his whole body was so sluggish and whacked out, that his every step was an effort, due to the long journey he had taken. When he finally came to the door, his first instinct was to hesitate before opening it, because he did not know what was on the other side. When he put his hand on the door's handle, he started to feel a tingling sensation and then he wrenched the door open, as far as it could go.

Then as he stepped outside, he saw an old book lying on the ground. As John was looking at it, its cover started to speak to him. It was saying "Open me". When John heard this he could not believe it, the cover actually spoke to him, that couldn't be true. Then it spoke again, "Open me". As John did so, a golden key was revealed, sparkling with a piercing brightness. John said, "Who are you?"

The key said, "Who do you think I am?"

As John looked round he saw that the door he came out of had vanished, and in its place was a small trap-door, so John tried the key in its lock. When he did so, a huge voice was heard from the trap-door. It said, "Who are you to disturb me?" Then, as if by magic, the door opened up fully.

Then as John looked inside, he could see nothing but mist and smoke, then as he went in further, he just made out a square stone with a chalice on top in the middle of the room. When he started to walk over to it, the chalice started to pulsate with a noise which was identical to a whale's singing noise. When John heard this, he became bemused and stunned by its wonderful harmonics.

Then he heard a little noise from outside, it was saying, "Don't leave me out here."

As John went outside he found the key on the ground. John said, "Was that you I heard?"

"Well it wasn't a ghost, was it?" the key replied.

John said, "Don't get sarcastic with me."

"Pick me up before I get rheumatism."

John said, "O.K., stop bickering."

Then as John picked him up he felt a huge draft behind him, as he looked round he saw that the room had disappeared. Then when he turned his head round to talk to the key, he found himself up against the tower.

In front of him was a set of stairs, and he trudged up these stairs along with his mate the key. It was John who decided to clear away all these obstacles that were confronting them, his fear of the tower and his lack of determination. Then as both of them got to the top level of the tower, they were astounded to find a thick protruding door with strange markings and two statues, one either side of the door. These statues were hand-carved, the key said, then John looked at the door markings to try and work out how to get inside. When he did so, one of the statues moved his head round as the key saw this, he shouted to John to look at the statue.

"Did you see it?" the key shouted.

"See what?" John said.

The key replied, "The statue, it moved on its own."

When John looked and touched the statue, it was as stiff as granite. Suddenly the statue moved, and started to spread a green liquid over the face of John.

When this happened John became temporarily blinded. As he put his hands to his face to try and clear away this liquid, his hands became entangled with it. While John was messing around with this liquid, the door in front of him started to open and a lone voice was heard in the distance. At this stage John was untangled out of his mess, he managed to wipe all the green away from his face, then he opened his eyes. John was still coming to terms with his blurred vision, as he began to focus properly on the figure standing in front of him. A very old man was standing there in his white robe and golden walking-stick outstretched in his hand. The old man then spoke, his voice was echoing, he was saying "For what purpose do you seek the secrets of the tower?"

When John heard this, he became puzzled, so he asked the

key for help. The old man shouted, "Are you the keeper or not!"

When John looked up in surprise he said, "Yes, I am the keeper of the tower."

Then as if by magic, John was put in a deep state of unconsciousness, and he was walking towards the old man in his deluded state. The old man was beckoning him on with his golden walking-stick. When the key witnessed this, he tried with all his might to wake his friend John from his unconscious state. He shouted to John, "Wake up!" If you don't, it will be the end of us."

Then the old man turned round and waved his stick at the ground, and as if by magic a golden throne had appeared out of nowhere. Then as the old man turned to John, he said, "Sit down on the throne, keeper of the tower."

When the key heard this he became frightened, and shouted to John not to sit down. Then suddenly John started to come out of his state of unconsciousness. After a couple of seconds John was wide awake. He said, "Where am I?"

When he saw where he was, he became frightened, then as he turned to face the old man, he was gone, he was nowhere to be seen. While he was looking round for the old man, the tower became weak in spirit and started to break up in front of him. When John saw the top ceiling falling down around him he started to run for his life, out into the corridor. He was confronted by the two statues, which had turned into little red devils with pitch-forks.

When the key saw this he became angry, he said to John "Let me deal with these."

John said, "Fine, all yours my little friend."

Then the key flew into the air, and started to twirl around and around. So they flung their forks at it, but the forks bounced off the key and headed back to the two devils and pierced them. The tower vanished, and John and the key were transported back to Hascon's fields. When the both of them realized where they were, they became overjoyed. After this they said their goodbyes to each other, and thus parted company to seek pastures new.

This was the story of the key and John. Who knows where it will lead them? Maybe to another Tower.

K5 Climb

The mountain ranges of the Pyrenees have always been a climber's fear – the fear of losing his life. This is a typical story, other tales have been and gone, but this one stays in the minds of those climbers who came to grief on the famous K5 mountain.

It all started when two climbers from England set out to climb the north face of K5. These two climbers were Chris Tolken and Adam Trench, experts in their fields. These two had climbed the north face of Everest, and the south face of K2. On the climb to Everest was where they met, and where Chris had the K5 climb in mind. While they were getting ready to climb the famous mount, Adam had sent down a helper to the local village to find a guide. He came across a famous guide called Tros Sanbeck. This was the climber who nearly conquered the Pyrenees, but the mountains nearly killed him in the process. When the helper asked Tros to guide for his masters, Tros replied, "For how much?" As the helper opened his wallet, Tros could see a load of gold coins, so Tros said "That will do", and took his gold coins.

The helper and Tros got about fifty yards up the road when an old man came out from behind a tree, and tried to warn them not to go any further with the climb. When Tros came up behind them he heard the old man warning them, he started to get apprehensive and frightened.

The old man went away, so the both of them carried on walking. A strange wind went by, it seemed to take their breath away. Tros asked himself if this was a bad omen, as they started up the hill to Chris and Adam at their base camp.

As they got within sight of Chris and Adam's camp, Tros was still thinking back to what the old man said, he was starting to get jumpy. When they eventually got to the base camp the helper said to Chris, "I think he's about to run off sir."

When Chris heard this he tried to persuade the guide to stay. For a while he was stubborn, then after a while he started to come round to their way of thinking. So they started on their climb to Wilson's peak, which was halfway to the summit, climbing and hoisting up their belongings. Chris was the first one to reach the jagged rocks of Wilson's peak. Then a couple of minute fragments seemed to break off near Adam, but Tros held on to him. When they got back to the edge of the mountain, they hoisted themselves up, and eventually got to Wilson's peak.

Chris had their tents up, as soon as the other two got into camp. A huge storm-cloud was brewing above them, and when they saw this all three rushed into their tents. A couple of seconds later the storm-cloud hit, both the tents were blown sideways. But Tros's tent got the full impact, it whipped his tent up with Tros inside, and down into a wide gorge. When his tent went down into the gorge his screams were drowned by the noise of the howling wind. This went on for a few hours, as the winds were smashing against the rocks outside. While this was going on, Chris and Adam were snuggled inside their sleeping bags.

They had not realized what the wind had done to Tros's tent. When a couple of hours went by, dawn was breaking outside, and also the weather was changing for the worse. By now it was snowing. As Chris ventured outside he saw to his horror that Tros's tent had been swept away. He shouted to Adam.

Then he noticed something on the ledge below the gorge. As Adam came out of his tent he said, "Be careful over there, or you will fall." When Chris got halfway down the gorge, he found Tros lying on a ledge, with his neck broken. So Chris shouted up to Adam to send down a long piece of rope. When Adam sent down the rope, Chris tied one end around Tros, and the other end around a rock that was sticking out, and then pulled. He then told Adam to pull up the other end of the rope. The rope began to thread itself along one of the jagged rocks that was pointing out from the rock face. When Adam saw this, he shouted down to Chris to hold on a second while he tried to re-loop the rope.

While Chris was waiting, with Tros's body, down below, he

was going back in time, to when Tros came to the camp, apprehensive about what the old man had said to him and the helper. Then a couple of seconds later, Adam shouted down, "Are you ready"

While Adam was pulling them up, the rope seemed to twang from the intense pressure that it was under.

Chris eventually got up the rock face with the body. While they were walking along the ridge to Wilson's peak, Chris said to Adam, "What shall we do with Tros's body?"

Adam said, "Wait till we get on to the peak, then we can bury him."

While they were resting, a loud rumbling was heard above them, as they looked up, they could not see anything so they got back to their rest. Then suddenly it hit them, a deafening barrage of rocks. While Chris was heading for cover, Adam got hit by a rock, and as he went down the avalanche covered him. While Chris was ducking under some cover he found his friend had died. When the deafening sound of the avalanche had ceased, Chris ventured out into the mass of rubble.

When he noticed a hand half-covered with rubble, Chris tried to lift the rocks off his friend, but this did not have any effect so he gave up. Chris said a little prayer over his departed colleague. He then said to himself, "This summit climb I am going to make will be a tribute to my fallen colleagues."

When he started to set off for the summit, he looked around him one more time, for sentimental reasons. Then as he was climb up and around the face, he came across a slippery ledge. As he put his foot on to it, his grip started to slip. Luckily, his foot got caught on a ridge which stopped him from falling down the mountain. Then as he climbed up again, he caught sight of a ledge above him, so he hoisted himself up.

A rumbling was heard above him. As Chris looked up he saw large fragments of rock bearing down towards him. As he hid for cover under a large jagged rock, he felt the rocks crashing against his cover. When a couple of seconds went by, he heard a silence. He poked his head out, and looked up. From where he was he could see the summit.

So he started on with his climb, hoisted up his body again, and dug his foot in, and climbed round the rock face. While he was doing this, he caught sight of the summit, which was twenty feet above him. When he saw this it spurred him on, so he hoisted himself up again, then a couple of seconds later he was at the summit. He then got out his Union Jack, and hit it into the ground on the summit. Chris shouted at the top of his voice, "Triumph at last!"

But at what cost?

Martian Incident

He was born in the year 1958, in the town of Sacramento, of a good family, though not of that country. His father came from Germany, and was a foreigner in this country, who settled here in the 1920s. His father had paved the way for him with a good education. After living in Sacramento for five years, his father married and became an American citizen. His name was Thomas, from whom his son was named Ben Thomas.

Sacramento was one of those ordinary towns where nothing seems to happen. For instance, drunks on the street, and music piping out from the cafes, and bright lights. In one of these cafes was a loft room where Ben Thomas lived. It was all he could muster with a teacher's salary. One night in September, one of the towns busiest periods, as Ben was marking his students' papers in his little loft room with all the bright lights flashing on and off, his eyes succumbed, and he took off his glasses for a rest. As he was rubbing his eyes, he felt a cold draft coming from the rear window. He noticed a strange blur out of the window as he put his glasses back on, a glowing ball hovering outside his window. When Ben saw this his whole frame turned to ice, like a frozen statue his eyes were glued to it. The intense heat forced him to look away, and as he did so the heat stopped. As he looked back he noticed a strange figure staring at him, and became frightened.

He ran for the door, and started to shout for help. While Ben was shouting, an old man was walking up the stairs from the cafe. When Ben saw the old man coming up, he shouted to him to have a look. The old man looked over to where Ben was pointing, he could see nothing. The old man said, "Look at what?"

The man thought Ben was nuts, but Ben explained, "Didn't you see it."

"See what?" the old man said.

It had vanished without a trace. Ben started shouting again, "We've been invaded!"

"Go back to sleep," the old man said. "I'm going home, you're nuts."

Ben sat down bemused. As the old man went downstairs, another man was coming up at the same time, and they both met in the middle of the stairs. The man called to Ben, "What was the matter?"

"He's nuts."

As Ben came to his senses, he went back into his room, and thought for a while on his bed, saying to himself, "What shall I do?"

"Right,' said Ben, "pack up all your belongings." As he was doing so, a strange sensation came over him, as if he were in a dazed state, and he fell back onto the wall. He noticed outside his rear window a red figure was looming, as Ben watched this figure its eyes seemed to penetrate into Ben's eyes.

The martian was trying to take him over and submit him to its will. Ben tried to look away, and as he did so the spell was broken. When Ben regained his proper self, he grabbed hold all his belongings and stormed down the stairs in a frenzy. When he got downstairs the cafe was full with people, and Ben tried dodging all the customers. As he was just getting to the street door, a drunk came out from nowhere and started to chat with Ben, who tried edging away from the drunk. As he did so, a strange silence came over the whole cafe, as if they had been frozen in time. As he got outside, the whole street was frozen in time.

When he got fifty yards down the street, an evil feeling came over him, as though he was being watched. When Ben looked up into the sky, he saw to his amazement a huge flying saucer, it was hovering over the town. Its presence was causing a wind-tunnel effect on the whole town, then suddenly the lights on the street blacked out. When Ben saw this it was the last straw, as he felt around the street for an open car to try to get away.

While he was looking, Ben was ducking down so as not to be seen by the martian. Then, as he was just giving up, he came across an open car, and as if by fate the lights came on. Without saying anything he just got in and drove as fast as he could out of town.

While he was driving along the empty road, he looked into

54

his front mirror and could see the whole town engulfed in a green mist. The flying saucer had laid siege to the town. When he got twenty-five miles out of town, he pulled over and stopped the car. When he got out of the car, opposite him was an old railway station. Ben ran down towards it, as he did so the flying saucer spotted him. He ran inside to look for cover, and came across a deep hole which was hollowed out. While he was looking over the hole, a gust of wind flew up from it, causing Ben to lose balance, and as he was trying to grab hold he fell in. As he was thrusting downwards into this black tunnel, his whole body was thrown into a chaotic state. After a couple of minutes, he came to rest on a wooden surface, where he came to after his long journey.

When Ben finally stood upright, all he could see was a hexagonal mirror hovering in the middle of the floor. The mirror opened up and swallowed Ben whole. He went down this deep chamber which had a gravitational pull, it was sucking Ben down and down into its core. Then as it was dragging him down, a gas was released from its outer wall. Ben could only hold his breath for thirty seconds. After that he would succumb to the gas, but while he was holding his breath a voice was heard from below saying, "Don't be afraid, all is okay."

After hearing that he fainted with shock, as he awoke he found himself in a white chamber with bright objects around him. A man was standing in the corner of the room, he was dressed all in red and as he spoke all his words were garbled. Then, as he was trying to communicate, he reached down to his waist, and a red button came on. "Where am I?" the martian said. It was coming out in English, Ben could not believe it.

Ben said, "Where is this chamber?"

The martian replied, "Inside my flying saucer. Don't be afraid. I will not harm you. I have been sent from a far-off galaxy, to see if any other life forms exist in this solar system."

While the martian had turned around to alter his controls, Ben rushed over to him to try and pull him away from the door. When he did so, the martian just disintegrated in front of him, and as Ben looked on the ground where the martian was, all he saw was a red cloak with ashes underneath. When he started to walk out of the door, a policeman was standing there.

Ben said, "What are you doing here?"

The policeman replied, "You're the one I should be saying that to."

When Ben looked round he was back in Sacramento, his face said it all. When the policeman asked Ben what he was doing here, Ben could not answer, he was still stunned. Ben said to himself "Was it a dream, or was it true?"

The policeman said, "Can you get into my car, please sir. I'd better take you down to the station for questioning."

When Ben got in, he was still talking to himself, as they started back to Sacramento, the policeman said, "What did you see?"

Ben said, "I don't know."

When they arrived on the outskirts where the police station was, Ben could not believe it, the town was just the same as if nothing had happened. When they pulled up outside the police station, another policeman was standing outside to escort him into the cells. When he put Ben into the open cell, Ben said, "That was strange, no lock on the door."

Then as he sat down on the bench, everything went bright. As he covered his eyes, a voice rang out. "So you thought you had got away from me." Then it started to laugh, it was so loud the walls began to vibrate and crack.

Ben replied, "I want to be a free man, not a prisoner."

Then as he was just going to run out of the door, a huge barrier came down in front of him, closing off his escape route. Ben said, "Where are you taking me?"

The martian did not answer. Ben then said, "Where was Sacramento? If it wasn't there at the start, was it destroyed? Was that Sacramento that I was in at the start?"

Ben's mind was playing tricks on him. Then he said, "Were they the real policeman at the start, or were they just martians dressed up, to look like real policemen. Or was this just a figment of my imagination, and did we really go for a ride in his police car, or was that false as well?"

Then as he was going over his thoughts, he noticed down on the floor something shiny. As he picked it up, a loud voice said, "Don't touch that, BEN!" Everything went black as he got up off the bench. The light came on he found himself in an old alley, as he started to walk up the alley his memory was coming back. He could see traffic going by, then as he got to the end of the alley he found himself in the real Sacramento this time. Ben could not believe it, as he got out on the street he screamed for joy, and everybody looked round with amazement. Ben said to himself, "I've beaten you." Then he said, "Or have I?" with his eyes looking up into the sky. "Who knows what lies ahead?"

Phoenix Triangle

The year was 1955, and the place was Florida, in the everglades. This story depicts a journey taken by a captain and his two nephews into the realms of the unknown, to untap the ancient mysteries which lay out to sea. It all started in late March, the captain had just bought his new boat from a trapper in the everglades. It had cost him his hard-earned cash, which he had worked for in the Florida Marina, modifying all the old boats.

When the captain started off down the everglades, his first stop was to pick up his nephews who were playing along the embankment. He cruised down the river, observing all the different creatures and rare forest still untouched. Then suddenly there was a jolt, and the captain found himself jammed on the embankment with his two nephews looking over him and laughing to themselves. He shouted to them, "Come on, get in, we're going on a mystery tour, a tour of the high sea and all its deep secrets."

So when the two nephews got into the boat, the captain started off down the everglades slowly threading his boat around the obstacles in the river. When he had got round the last obstacle in the river, the sea wall was only 300 yards away in the distance, the captain could just about see it glinting in the sunlight.

Then as they neared the sea wall, the captain shouted to the two nephews to get down below inside the boat for safety reasons. Outside the sea wall the sea was rough and a strange sea was sweeping up over the calm tidal waves, altering the sea's magnetic fields. When the captain saw this he did not know whether to halt, or carry straight on regardless. Then as he ventured out to sea with his nephews, his boat got eighty yards out when his motor gave out, leaving him helplessly drifting. The sea at this time was moving into a force-eight gale. The captain tried to force his little craft away from the core of the storm. His boat at this time was going up and down like a yo-yo, coasting through the waves. He went outside to check his nephews. As he was walking along the boat's ledge, he was suddenly hit by a plank of wood from the treacherous sea. As the wooden plank hit the captain's head, he became unbalanced and was slipping off the ledge, unable to hold on.

When he fell he landed safely on the outer ledge, then as a couple of seconds had gone by the captain was slowly regaining his senses. Then as he looked up he saw what looked like a brown shape on his lap, then he tried rubbing his eyes to get a clearer view. As he opened his eyes again, he found that the piece of wood was on his lap covered in seaweed, then as he scraped off the seaweed it showed a warning. It said "Do not go on with this journey", so when the captain saw this he became apprehensive, and his nerves at this time were jangling with tension. Then without any warning the plank just sprang back into the sea, leaving no trace of ever being there on the boat, only the coldness of a strange wind.

The sea had become calm and still as though nothing had happened. When he looked out to sea, he saw what looked like a ship on the horizon, and the captain stood upright and went inside his cabin to fetch his binoculars. Then when he ventured outside and put his binoculars up to his eyes to have a closer look, he found to his horror that the ship was drifting with nobody on board. When he saw this he went downstairs to tell his nephews what he had seen on the deck. As he got twenty yards away from the cabin, where the two nephews were playing, a huge thump was heard up top, so the captain turned around and started up the stairs. He had forgotten his two nephews, so he shouted to them to stop playing and to come up on deck. Something was wrong.

The ship had drifted alongside his boat. It was worn with age and creaking with all the many voyages it had undertaken during its lifetime. Then as he glanced up to one of the two masts he saw a plaque half hanging off, it said, "This is the Phoenix Triangle." It was the largest tall ship he had ever seen, and imprinted on its side was the date 1798. It was over one hundred and fifty years old. The captain said to himself, "Where has it been all this time."

Then as he was glued to this sight, his two nephews came up

the stairs and jumped on its hanging ropes which were drifting in the water. When the captain glanced down from the ship he could not believe his eyes, he shouted to them, "Get out of there otherwise you'll hurt yourselves!"

When the nephews heard this, instead of getting off they carried on with their swinging, then one of the ropes snapped. When this happened the closest nephew tried to grab hold of the other, then they both fell in together into the cruel sea. Without wasting a second, the captain dived in. While he was thrashing his way through the waves, the nephews were battling to save themselves from drowning and going under from exhaustion. The waves were reaching peak height, then as the captain swam with all his might, he caught a glimpse of the boys.

He shouted to them to swim over to him, but it was no good because the next moment a giant wave came over and the captain was overcome with water. After a couple of seconds the captain resurfaced. Then when he looked around him the boys had disappeared without trace, all he could see were huge waves bouncing against each other and himself bobbing up and down in the sea. Suddenly he caught sight of the Phoenix Triangle, it was drifting towards him. When the captain saw this he became stricken with panic and paralyzed with fright.

A feeling of desperation set in, then without wasting any time he slowly came to his senses. When he saw the ship still heading towards him, he swam for all his worth, but it was no good, the ship was increasing in speed. He stopped and closed his eyes in exhaustion.

The captain opened his eyes only to see the ship drifting by him, so he grabbed at the nearest dangling rope and held on for dear life, not knowing where the ship was taking him, whether it be the unknown regions of hell. His fate was with the ship, as he was being dragged through the cruel cold sea, his memory going back to the time he was coasting around the everglades without a care in the world.

The sea was increasing in ferocity, and as the captain came out of his motionless state, he found himself slipping under the oncoming waves. He was saying to himself, "I can't hold on for much longer." The feeling of drowning came over him, then with the next second he put all his strength into climbing the rope. As he tried his fingers were so wet that they couldn't grab hold properly, and he kept slipping down each time he tried. He tried grabbing another piece of rope, which was also dangling in the sea. As he climbed the tense rope he found that his fingers began to bleed and were badly bruised with all the pushing and pulling of the rope, then as he reached the top deck he could see that the ship was deserted.

He tore off a bit of his shirt to put round his bleeding hands, then after he had bound them he glanced up and saw a silvery figure standing under the bridge. As the captain walked towards him, the silvery figure saw him and started down the stairs to the gallery. The captain got to the stairway and found it deserted, then he said to himself "I will take a big chance and venture down to see if I can find him again." As he started down these winding stairs he noticed something strange, a white mist was flowing down the stairs at the same time.

He also noticed that it was twirling around his legs, like a snake encircling him, twisting and turning as it went. When the captain saw this he became frightened and started to back away from it. Then when the mist felt this turnabout in the captain, it started to disappear from sight, seeping underneath every nook and cranny and every little hole to hide. Then suddenly there was a huge crash and the captain was thrown headfirst to the slippery floor. He ran up the stairs to see what had happened outside. When he got out he found that the ship had drifted on to a sand ledge in the sea. As he looked out to sea, he saw a shore-line with a little cove, then as he looked back at the ship it was tilting at a forty-five degree angle.

When the captain felt this, his first thought was to jump in the sea, then as it tilted over some more there was no other choice, he had to dive in. The sudden cold when he dived in made him shiver all over his body, then he started swimming towards the shore. As he glanced up from the waves he could see a long figure standing on the beach.

The captain arrived on the beach and as he walked on the sand, he got about fifty yards up the beach when he caught sight of a hut. As the captain ventured over to it, he noticed that the door was very old because it still had its original brackets and locks. Then as he tried opening the door, it creaked open and all the dust that had accumulated on it flew off.

When the door opened the captain could see a man with his

back to him, so he shouted out to him saying, "Can you help me, I am lost."

All he got was silence. So the captain went over to him and put his hand on his shoulder, then as the figure turned round the captain got the fright of his life. The figure had no face. Then he spoke. "I am the keeper of the hut, what do you seek?"

When the captain heard this he ran out of the door as quickly as possible. A misty fog was covering everything in sight as the captain wandered through it. Then as he came out he was in a different location, he was standing on an old harbour still covered in seaweed. He looked up and saw the tall ship Phoenix Triangle.

When the captain stood on the harbour admiring this great feat, to his surprise his two nephews came up from behind him. When the captain saw them, he could not believe his eyes. He said, "Where have you been all this time? I was worried about you."

Then one of the nephews spoke saying, "Captain, we were sucked down this whirl-pool. Then as we awoke we found ourselves marooned on this island."

So the captain said to them, "Right let's get out of this place." They all got on the ship and set sail. Then as the captain started to adjust the steering he could not budge it, even when he tried levering with a piece of metal that he found on the deck. While this was going on up top, the nephews were playing down below in the corridor, as the ship veered over to the left then the right. The nephews were thrown headfirst down the slippery corridor. On deck a thick black fog was forming near the ship, making it hard for the captain to see. Then the nephews got up and ran out on deck to see what the commotion was all about.

As the nephews looked up to where their captain was, they found him still grappling with the steering wheel. Then as he stopped, he noticed that the fog had increased in speed and was just venturing on to the ship with the wrath of the gods. All of a sudden the ship stopped in the middle of nowhere. By this time the fog had engulfed the whole ship, it was a thick, black mucky fog, not like normal fog, a bit like tar. He tried shouting down at the nephews, saying "Are you O.K. down there?"

There was no answer, so he ran down to see where they were.

62

Then as he got down the stairs, everything was empty. He heard a clanging sound coming from the port side of the ship, so he walked slowly through the fog and found when he got there that the clanging sound was his boat brushing against the side of the ship, covered in seaweed and with his two nephews in it already. The captain said, "Why didn't you answer me?" then they looked at him and laughed. The captain jumped into the boat, he said to them, "Wait till I get you home", then he steered away from the Phoenix Triangle.

Then as he got fifty yards away from it, he saw it tilt over and down it went to the depths of the unknown, throwing up huge bubbles as it went down. The captain ventured over to its last position to look for wreckage. Then as he got near, he saw a plaque floating on the surface and bent down to pick it up from the sea. He noticed that it had some writing on it, it said "This was the Phoenix Triangle, the last great tall ship put to rest", then as he was holding the plaque it vanished without a trace. While he was looking around for it, his nephews were looking out to sea and chatting to themselves. He said, "Come on you two, look for the plaque."

Then as he got no answer from them, he went over to them to see what the matter was. As he turned them around, they had no faces. When he saw this he screamed, then he fainted. As the minutes and hours went by, he slowly came to out of his collapsed state, to find he was the only one on his boat, alone and frightened. A flash of lightning crashed down on to his deck, and a voice said, "So you thought you had got away with it, haha! For this is 1789, and not 1955." The captain was left in a paralyzed state, not knowing what to do, so he got out his journal and wrote in it: "This is the captain speaking from the boat Wilson, help me please, because I am from the future. This is the log."

The Expedition

The place was Egypt, the time was 1864. A European ship had decked inside the town's harbour, to take on provisions and fuel for its long journey back. This ship was no ordinary craft, it was the holder of many strange fossils, ancient relics found off the Crison Delta covered in a strange capsule.

A famous party of explorers had been sent from England to try and retrieve the Crison Star, which had been missing for many hundreds of years. This star was the only thing missing from the consignment of relics, its last location was found to be near the Crison Delta. When the captain saw its location on the map – it was situated in unknown waters – his reaction was amazement tinged with fear. Then as he was going to open his cabin door, a knock was heard, then as he opened it the two explorers were standing there as if by fate. When the captain saw them he said, "Come in gentlemen, I was just on my way to get you, to ask about the location."

Then one of the explorers spoke, he said, "My name is John Barton and my friend's name is Sasan Hampton. What is your question Captain?"

The captain said, "My question is, how long do we have to stay in these waters, because so many other ships have gone down in these strange tidal waters."

"We knew how difficult it was going to be, so we have devised a shorter route for you."

When the captain looked at this he became bemused. He said, "This is even worse."

The other explorer said "Why?", then the captain said, "Because it takes us near the Crison Delta."

John Barton said, "That is the best that we can do considering the circumstances.

Then Sasan said, "Sorry."

When the captain heard this he said, "OK then, but we

must watch out for the strange waters."

So the ship set sail, this time for the Crison Delta. Two days went by, the waters were calm, then out of nowhere it began to change for the worse. A strange storm was seen from the crows nest. As they drew closer to the storm, they could feel strange electrical jolts around them. It was also turning the sky red, then it had turned orange with mauve patches. The captain said this was very unusual. Then a couple of seconds later a sharp flash was felt all over the ship. It was making the ship blow, and the flashes were getting brighter with every hit. As the ship started to turn out of the storm, a loud thunder was heard from the clouds, then as they passed all the way through it all stopped.

Then as they started to move, a strong sea-rage was pulling the ship towards a solid mass which was stationary in the sea. As the ship drew up alongside it, the two explorers ran up the ship to get a better look at this monolith in the sea. They could hear it humming. When they heard this the two explorers could not believe what they were hearing, then the captain shouted down, "Hold on to something, there's a big wave coming towards us."

Then as one of the explorers looked up, he said, "Oh my God!" As the wave hit, everything was flung into the sea, then as they came up they could see that the ship had turned over and was sinking. They shouted out to the captain, but it was no good, there was nothing but silence and a weird feeling of emptiness that had settled inside them.

Then as they were bobbing up and down in the cruel sea, they could see the monolith still solid, so they started to swim over to it. While they were swimming, they kept seeing bright flashes in front of their eyes. Then as they touched it, they both went unconscious, and when they awoke, they found themselves covered with sand and drenched in sea water, lying on a deserted beach.

When they awoke fully, they noticed that the sea was red in colour and had large whirlpools sucking in huge amounts of water, and afterwards it spat it out like a whale blowing out its air. A loud bang was heard behind them, and as they turned round they could see a light flickering on and off. When the two explorers saw this their curiosity got the better of them, so they walked over to the entrance of the cave where the light was flickering. As they walked into this cave, their eyes caught sight of a strange humming bird perching on this black solid mass which was pulsating with intense ferocity. Suddenly the bird began to change colour, then as if by magic it changed into a star. John Barton said, "Do you know what that is?"

When Sasan looked up he said, "Oh no! It is the Crison Star."

The famous star which had been missing all these years spoke to them, saying "Who are you to enter my palace!"

Then John Barton said, "We seek the star."

"You are brave to utter those words, or foolhardy. Which is it?"

John said, "The latter."

When the star heard this he said, "You are straightforward, I like that. The star you seek holds many dangers so beware, because you may come unstuck if you are not careful."

Then as they started to move towards it they were stopped in their tracks. John shouted "I can't move!" then Sasan said the same thing.

Then the star spoke again. "As I predicted, you had evil thoughts in your mind. The star knows everything, did you think you would get away with it"

Then suddenly a bright glow was seen drawing nearer and nearer, when the two explorers saw this they shouted "Help us!" then it said, "You knew your fate when you passed through that door."

The two of them turned to each other, and said "What shall we do?"

John said, "Close your eyes and pray, and I will do the same thing."

Then, as the glow got right up to them, they fainted. When they came to, they found themselves near the monolith. They closed their eyes and opened them again. Their location had changed again, this time it was a deserted cave-mine with water dripping from the roof. They shouted up the cave but nothing was heard, then as they were on the verge of moving, an echo came back saying, "See you in hell." When they heard this, they started to run for their lives and found themselves in a state of slow motion. Even their voices were slurred. John said, "We have entered a warp flux, what shall we do?"

Sasan said, "Just flow with it, because it could be dangerous to try and alter it in motion."

Then all of a sudden it stopped. When they came out of it, they found themselves in an all-white room with a round ball in the middle. When they went over to it they could see pictures of their past and their present, but not the future. John said, "I wonder why, maybe it's trying to tell us something."

Sasan said, "I hope not, I want to live."

"So do I," said John.

Then out of nowhere a burst of energy erupted out of the ball, causing the ball to disintegrate. They tried to get out, but to no avail. As the energy grew stronger, so did its heat ratio, John's face at this stage was blistering under the heat, as was Sasan's face. John shouted, "I can't take too much of this, it's burning me up."

Sasan at this stage had fainted, then as a couple of seconds went by the heat stopped in one instant. While they were out cold, a series of events passed by them, then as they came to they noticed that they were on a ship out at sea. They stood up and looked over the bows, feeling drowsy after their long voyage.

Then as John opened his right hand, he found the star of the delta. He said, "How did I get this? Why didn't he kill us? Heaven knows." When he looked down again the star was gone. John said, "Have you seen it Sasan?"

He said, "No, where did it go? Maybe to the far side of the earth where the unknown is situated, or maybe hell took it out of spite."

Cumulus and the Four Keys

This story is taken from an ancient old book which has been handed down by generations that have gone before. This is one of those old stories, as we begin we find Cumulus working out to sea on a ship, one of those sailors who did not know his left arm from his right. But this did not stop him from learning the ropes. As he was threading his first knot, he was startled by a looming shadow which was hovering above him. Then as Cumulus looked up, he saw a winged serpent. It came out of the sun, the glare was too much so Cumulus shielded his eyes. At that moment the winged serpent dived down towards the ship, and as Cumulus looked at it four keys dropped into his lap.

As he felt this, he shouted with fright, "What does this mean?", then as all the ship's company looked, they could not believe their eyes. Then suddenly with a flash he was gone, the serpent had vanished without a trace. As the four keys were lying on Cumulus's lap, his balance on the rigging became impaired with all the commotion. Then suddenly he lost his footing and fell overboard, but as he was accelerating towards the sea, something out of the ordinary happened, a gust of wind got underneath Cumulus and floated him down on to the ship. He shouted to the captain, "Look sir," and as the captain did he could not believe what he was seeing.

A huge bubbling noise was heard coming from the side of the ship, and Cumulus and the rest of the crew went over to see what it was. As the captain came through, a huge roar rang out. Like a huge volcano it erupted, up it came like a towering inferno, a huge beast with long fangs, then suddenly its form began to change into a roman centurion.

It loomed over the ship and said, "Do not seek the four golden doors, everything is against you. Beware, for time is short."

68

Then it slowly sank into the sea, still looking at them as it sank without trace. Suddenly the rush of water banged against the ship, making it unbalanced and dangerously tilted, taking on water heavily.

Then for an instant Cumulus saw a bright flash in front of his eyes, and he saw the four keys tied to a unicorn. Then as a couple of seconds went by, he came back to his original self. Suddenly the captain grabbed the keys off Cumulus and said, "Who gives you the right to have these?"

Then as the captain was looking at them, the keys began to glow and a fireball erupted out of the captain. The captain was left as a pile of ashes on the deck, still smouldering, and lying on top were the four keys. As Cumulus picked them up, the keys spoke, saying, "Never let me out of your hands again. That man was wrong, stand up for yourself in future."

When Cumulus heard this he dropped the keys in amazement.

Then as Cumulus, for the second time, picked up the keys from the deck a loud vibration was heard underneath the ship. Cumulus shouted out "What is that!"

The keys said, "Jump overboard quickly, there is no time to lose."

As they did so, the ship disappeared in a puff of smoke, leaving poor old Cumulus and the keys out in the deep blue sea, all alone to face the elements.

After a couple of days, the two of them were still floating. Cumulus at this time was on the verge of going under, when the key shouted out, "Land ho!", then as Cumulus looked up, there it was.

Cumulus shouted out, "Lord, at last we've made it!"

In a frantic effort, he paddled for all his worth. Then gradually the land got nearer and nearer, and at last they reached the shore, but as they swam up, the shoreline was out of the ordinary. The strange crust on the surface bore the telltale signs of movement underneath, and also a weird buzzing sound.

Then suddenly out of the sky a giant bee dived down, as Cumulus saw this terrifying sight he ran. As he was running with the keys, and without him knowing, behind him the keys started to glow, then with an almighty bang, a ray of light came out of this tiny key and destroyed the attacking bee.

When Cumulus stopped and looked round, the bee was nowhere to be seen. Then as he reached into his back pocket, the key at this time had changed back to its original colour. "Thank you," said Cumulus, "you have saved my life."

They started on their journey to search for the four doors. Then as they had walked a few hundred yards, they noticed in the distance a mist with tornadoes inside it. As they got nearer, Cumulus was fascinated, he could not take his eyes off it. As Cumulus and the keys were just a few yards away, a huge sandstorm raced up, making a closed door behind them.

Suddenly from the mist came a big face with horns around his forehead saying, "Who are you to defile my territory?"

Then the keys said, "The keeper of the doors." As the face heard this he started to laugh, and the earth began to shake under the vibration. The face lowered his breath and exhaled a fireball, and the key put up an invisible barrier in front of them. Cumulus at this time had his hands up to his face and was kneeling on the ground praying. As the keys looked down they said, "Get up you fool, and have faith in us next time."

The keys just had enough time to recharge their energy pack, then they let rip. The power that came out was phenomenal. As Cumulus shielded his eyes from the glare, within a second it was gone, the face and mist were no more to be seen. Then as a couple of seconds went by, everything around them went black. Cumulus shouted, "Where are you?"

The keys said, "Over here, quick, I've found something.

Cumulus said, "Hold on, I'm coming, don't rush me I'm going as fast as I can in the circumstances."

Then as Cumulus looked up, even the sky was blacked out. Then as he went on another step, he came across the keys. They were embedded into a wall, but it was no ordinary wall.

The keys said, "Mind how you go, just pretend I'm not here." Then he tried to pull them out of the wall. Nothing happened. But it was no good, Cumulus tried with all his might to hold on to the keys, but it was no good, still the force was pulling them into the wall.

A giant forcefield was reacted, it slowly started to suck everything in sight, including Cumulus, who tried digging his fingernails into the ground. But his effort was insignificant, and poor old Cumulus was sucked into the cauldron of vibrating air pockets. Then from nowhere a giant plant root tied itself around him, making it impossible for him to move or even twitch, then as Cumulus was trying to free himself, he banged his head on the solid branch that was threading itself around his head. While he was unconscious the wall took him on a long journey.

Then as he came round from his bump on the head, he gradually opened his eyes to view the greatest sight of his entire life, a treasure trove laden with riches beyond belief. As he went round looking, he noticed a rustling in one of the trunks, so as Cumulus went over to it to open it, he heard a noise saying "Get me out of here."

Then as he got the keys out of the trunk, he looked round to find four doors in front of him, saying above them, "Come in, at your own risk". As Cumulus stood paralyzed not knowing which one to take, the keys said "Take any one."

"No, it might lead us to disaster,' cried Cumulus.

"Try either one then, otherwise we will be here for ever," cried the keys. He put his key into the lock of the first door, and nothing happened. Then as Cumulus tried the next door, the key in the lock was turning around and around. Cumulus said, "Stop!"

"I can't!" screamed the key.

Suddenly if by magic, the turning of the key stopped. Cumulus tried to pull the key out of the first door but it would not come out. He sat down for a rest, and a strange noise was heard from the other side of the door. When Cumulus heard this he lifted himself off the floor in great haste, bewildered as to the nature of the sound.

Cumulus said to himself, "What could this be?", then the key flew out of the lock, and landed in his arms. The noise grew louder and more deafening in pitch, as Cumulus looked round and put his hands to his ears to cut out the sound. Suddenly a voice said, "Who are you to disturb my sleep? This is my world, who gives you the right to interfere?"

The key shouted at him, "Who the hell are you to tell us?"

"I am the lawgiver here!" shouted the third door.

"Haven't I seen you somewhere before?"

Cumulus replied "No."

"Yes, I thought I had," cried the third door, "I was the winged serpent who dropped these keys into your lap. I thought I recognized you."

As the door opened up, lo and behold, the inner thoughts of Cumulus's past were on show around the whole perimeter of the door. Then as the two of them entered the room inside, it started to shudder.

Cumulus shouted, "What is happening?"

The key said, "Look out, it's falling down."

As Cumulus ran to get out the way, another piece of falling masonry broke off the ceiling and fell directly onto poor old Cumulus's head. Suddenly, he was knocked to the ground. As he lay there, his eyes glazed with concussion, fading into a state of sleep, he saw the faint shape of a human being.

Then as he was just falling into his sleep, a voice said, "Count to three and all will be well, and tap your heels together three times." Then as Cumulus did this, he awoke to find himself on his ship's mast, at the start of his journey. And in his hand was a battered old key. "Am I free?" shouted Cumulus at the top of his voice.

Then a huge gathering of clouds came over the ship. They stopped over it, and said, "You wish!" For we hold the power."

"Help me!" came the cry from Cumulus.

Obelisk

The word obelisk comes from the Greek word obelos meaning dagger-shaped. These ancient monuments were regarded as symbols of the Egyptian art, and thought to have strange mystical powers given from the sun gods from the caves of Syene. These old stone monoliths were driven into the ground, and raised up with ropes and jacks. When erected in its sacred position, the whole stone was covered with writings and hieroglyphics. These went through centuries of huge change, but to present day they still have not been touched or tampered with, due to the strange hypnotic powers they possess.

This is one story which altered that. It happened on a dreadful day in late October in the year of our lord 1938. The man involved was Dr Shaffer a geologist, whose fascination with the Egyptian Obelisk brought him to far-off Egypt, to see what strange hypnotic power it had.

Dr Shaffer started his journey travelling through the wastelands of the desert. When he got twenty-five miles out in the desert, he stood a while on the dunes looking around him to see which was the best way to go. Then as he looked down at the map which he had in his hand, a strange noise was heard in the distance. Dr Shaffer put away his map and ventured over to where this noise was coming from, then he noticed the strangest thing, a sand whirlpool was whirling around and around. Suddenly the force of it started to drag him in.

When Dr Shaffer felt this, his first instinct was to lean back and stop himself from being dragged in. But it was no good, the force was too strong. He clambered through the sand trying to hold on to his grip and his footing, but the next moment he was sucked in, careering down a tunnel of death. He was surprised to find that there was air down here. Then suddenly out of nowhere, a white smoky mist was drifting up the tunnel. When the doctor saw this, he tried to climb up, grabbing at every spike which was sticking out of the walls. He tried to save himself from being overcome by the mist, but as he tried the mist was increasing its speed with every second and it was all in vain. The next moment he was overcome, then as the mist slowly drifted through his body it caused a change in his muscular structure, and left its mark with dire consequences.

Then after a few seconds had passed by, the doctor's body had changed out of all recognition, and the draft of air was decreasing in force. While all this was going on inside the walled tunnel, down below in the chambers lay the oldest obelisk ever recorded. It had lain undisturbed for thousands of years hidden in the inner regions, surrounded by granite rock and secret passages preserved throughout time. Then as the doctor drifted down to the ground, he became embroiled in emotion by the sight of his body all disjointed and indistinguishable. Then as he was kneeling, in front of him was a see-through mirror. As the doctor glanced into it, he saw what looked like a person with his head turned. Then as the doctor got even closer, the head turned all the way round and to the doctor's horror, it was himself aged about fifty years.

As he saw these grim features, he fainted with fright and landed face down on the ground. While he was drifting, the surroundings around him were changing. The change which was taking place was to the earth's magnetic fields, creating a dip in the earth's core making the planet a dangerous place for all mankind. While all this was going on, the doctor was awaking from his collapsed state and glanced up to find his mirror had changed into a field of static blue lights, which was holding back a sea of compressed water. As he noticed this, he slowly got to his feet and ventured over to it to have a closer look. As he did so, a strange feeling came over him as if a foreign body had been placed inside his body, then as he hesitated for a moment to retrace his thoughts.

The sea wall started to shake, then as the doctor looked up from his state of motionlessness, he saw what looked like a mutant of some kind. He jumped into the wall, only to be confronted by a pack of mutant men as he came out on the other side. Then when they took one look at him, they realized he was one of them but in reverse, so they grabbed hold of him and slowly put a mask over him to stop him from drowning in the sea. The pressure of the sea was causing his cheeks to sink into his face, with a frozen outer skin and a cold disjointed face in a frost-bitten state.

By all accounts he should have died in the sea, because the sea was at that temperature where only the thick-skinned ventured into the deep. Then as the doctor and mutants finally came out of the sea, in front of them was a tall monolith. It was the OBELISK. When the doctor saw this he became paralyzed with shock. Then as he stood in the frozen sea, still dumbfounded by the strange sight in front of him, a floating mud was drifting near him. When the mutants looked round they became erratic with fear, because the mud was their enemy, so they started backing away. When the doctor caught sight of the floating mud, he tried swimming away from it with a frontcrawl stroke towards the shoreline. Then as he looked round for a second, the mud had increased its speed and was just about to pounce on him.

A huge roar went up, then out of nowhere a bolt of laser lightning came from the monolith and struck the mud. After a few seconds there was no mud, it had disintegrated without trace. All that was left were a few bubbles bouncing up and down in the sea. Then as he looked round to thank the obelisk, it had also vanished, and to his surprise he was in his own back yard in England.

The Witch's Domain

Many myths and legends have been told and written, but this one is different. Because this one has the stinging touch, it tells of a witch's domain untouched for thousands of years until now.

According to the legend there were three witches, each of whom possessed a lethal power unknown in origin. Now it came to pass in the sixtieth year, in the month of September, a unique boy was born. This boy when he was born had the mark of Zeus impregnated on his right hand. HE WAS THE ONLY THING THAT STOOD IN THE WAY OF THE DARKNESS.

As the years rolled by, the boy grew into a man. This man was named Issac, his livelihood was fishing. One day as he was out fishing as usual, he noticed something entangled in his line. When he tried to pull it in Issac became apprehensive, because one day when he was a boy, he went fishing with his father out in the cove, and as they were pulling in their catch the line had become entangled. As his father went to free it, a huge black figure pulled him into the sea below. When Issac went to help his father, all he saw when he got there were bubbles floating on the surface.

When Issac reached down into the sea, he began to feel something really cold, like an ice cube. Then suddenly it lurched up at him with a vengeance, and as it grabbed hold of him the figure said, "Your time is coming, my young boy." Then it vanished without a trace, and Issac stood bewildered and stunned. This time when he started to reel in his line, he saw a dark figure emerging from the depths of the sea. As he saw this coming up, Issac took hold of one of his oars. When it finally surfaced Issac hit it with all his might, but it did not move. Issac was astounded.

When he finally stopped hitting it, he looked down to see

how it was. As he did so he started to laugh, the thing was a lump of seaweed. While he was laughing a huge burst of escaping gas was blown out of the sea, and he stopped laughing to look at this strange phenomenon. Then as the surface went back to normal, Issac looked round to his oars to start back to shore. While he was doing this, a bright light was beamed up from the place where the gas had blown. When Issac saw this, he could not take his eyes off it, and as he was watching this a black figure was forming inside the light. Issac could just make out the appearance of an old woman, then a voice was heard. "Come into the light," it was saying. When Issac heard this he began to get frightened. When he tried to break away, another light came out of nowhere and started to pull Issac's boat into the beam of light where the figure was.

Issac tried to jump overboard, when he did so he found to his horror that the light was solid. This solid light was all round the boat, Issac was trapped, then as the boat was coming up to the figure, it stopped dead. In an instant the figure's beam began to open up, and a witch-like figure was seen. The figure spoke, saying, "You want to know about the Witch's Domain. Come, I will show you to the mysterious unknown. While they were travelling through the gates of hell, Issac noticed a plaque saying "The one who seeks danger, seeks the Witch's Domain."

When he saw this his whole body began to tremble with fear. While he was gazing into the unknown, looking at all the light's zooming past him, with such speed and unique sharpness, Issac said to himself "Am I going to follow my father, or am I going to live another day?" Then suddenly they came to an abrupt end, in front of them was a large cave, its entrance illuminated with an evil light.

Then as the witch went inside, Issac was deliberating whether to go in or not, as he stood outside for a moment. A huge roar rang out from the darkness, when he heard this Issac ran inside the cave as fast as he could. When he got inside, he saw three witches with three rods of glistening brightness, holding hands forming a circle. They were chanting, and also forming a triangle with the three rods that they had in their hands. To his surprise they turned around and glared at him. In an instant, their eyes came alive, and out of their six sockets came a twirling and threatening green monster. When it proceeded towards Issac, he put his arms in a criss-cross position in front of him. When Issac did this, the mark of Zeus was exposed, making the monster retreat. As it did so, Issac to his amazement found himself still alive.

When Issac began to take down his arms from his face, he noticed that the monster had retreated back into the witches' eye-sockets. Issac said to himself "Why did it retreat?" Suddenly he looked down at his arm, it was glowing with the sign of Zeus. Then he said, "That's why."

Then all he heard was a piercing noise coming from the place where the witches were standing. When Issac glanced over to the place where the noise was coming from, he put his hands up to his ears in distress. The noise was so deafening that it made his ears bleed. When Issac felt this he began to run out into the darkness.

While he was out in the darkness, with his hands still clasped over his ears, he found himself transported back to prehistoric times. He could hear the noises of the wild animals, and the echoes from the mountain ranges. When he started to walk, his path was taking him through all kinds of strange plant life, all abnormal in size. Then as he walked on about thirty yards he came across a huge toadstool. As he bit off a piece, it tasted like a very old piece of furniture. Then as Issac was eating this, he became aware that something was watching him out of the bushes.

Then all of a sudden, he heard this strange noise coming from the bushes. As he went to investigate, a strange feeling started to come over him. He tried to focus properly with his eyes as they became more blurry. He walked forward a few steps and came into contact with a sharp object. Issac was laid out unconscious. His mind began to play tricks on him, he found himself going around and around, it was having a strange effect on him. When he was dreaming and fighting against his subconscious, his whole system was taking a battering, he began to sweat and shout out. When a couple of hours went by, Issac became still, then as he started to come out of it he found himself in a white chamber.

When Issac finally awoke out of his dream, above him were three mirrors. As he stood up he saw to his disgust and horror, the three witches bearing down on him. When Issac said to the witches "What do you want with me?", they replied, "We seek to destroy you."

"Why?" said Issac.

"You have the mark of Zeus."

Then suddenly Issac's arm began to react to the mark, within a few seconds his whole arm was covered with bumps and sores. When the witches saw this happening, they began to panic, they were talking amongst themselves, saying "What is happening to him?"

Then as the arms grew, Issac fell down with the agonizing pain, as it was pulsating with redness, Issac became unconscious. Then all of a sudden Issac's arm burst open, and out came a living organism. When the witches saw this, they started to build up their lethal power. As they put their bright rods together, out came a power which was awesome.

When they directed it at the living organism, it started to react by increasing its outer seal. When the build-up was overflowing, the witches let go of their potent force, which came speeding towards the organism. The organism just stood there dormant, as the light hit it seemed to bounce off its shell.

The light came back at the witches at full strength. The force was so strong that it cracked the three mirrors, transporting two of the witches into the phantom zone, sealing them for all eternity. While all this was going on, Issac had just come out of his unconsciousness. When he began to awake fully, he saw to his amazement the thing next to him was changing form, and Issac began to edge away. When he did so, the living organism began cracking open, releasing all the air that was trapped inside.

When all the air was out, the thing seemed to change colours. Then in a split second, something was starting to emerge out of the shell, with human characteristics. Then the last of the witches came out of her mirror, to where the living organism was. In doing so, the witch was conserving energy. At this time, Issac was caught between the two of them, then finally the organism became a man. When Issac saw what was formed, he could not believe that it had come out of his arm. Then as the last witch was raising her rod to the organism, it retaliated, and as it did so both were encapsulated within the power of the phantom zone.

When Issac saw this he shielded his eyes with his arms. Then he heard a loud bang in the distance. He found himself drifting in the sea, holding a piece of old driftwood. Imprinted on it was this: "The domain has ceased, the danger has passed, you have destroyed the three witches." Then as he looked down at his arm, Issac saw the mark of Zeus fade. Instead came his father's name, with the message: "Godspeed, all is well, the organism was me."

Archway to Hell

Many centuries ago in a far-off land, steeped in myths and fables, stood a wooden spike that was covered in blood, the blood of a dead soul. This was the tradition which was handed down through the ages. Tradition also says that a book was left next to the spike to ward off evil spirits, and this book was called Archway to Hell. Then as the centuries flew by, the book was never seen again until now, in the hidden wastes of Egypt. We begin in a tomb near the Valley of the Kings, where two scientists were working. Dr Arnold and Dr Sandra Hines had come from the Egyptology centre of ancient archives. As we begin the first day we find the doctors hard at work down the tomb. As Dr Hines was shifting some sand from one of the tomb's walls, she came across a small pile of hardened sand, between the wall and the floor of the tomb.

Then as the doctor started to scrape out this hardened sand, a strange thing happened. A swift movement was heard below them under the floor, it seemed to jump from left to right, then stop. Doctor Hines said "I don't like this, let's get out of here." But it was too late. As they started to move, the sand in the middle of the tomb started to sink inwards, and created a quicksand. When they felt this, Doctor Arnold tried pushing his colleague out of the sand, but to no avail. Then as a last ditch effort to reach the outer step of the tomb, Dr Arnold tried reaching over to a piece of cloth which was hanging out of one of the walls.

But as he reached over to it, his own weight pulled the cloth out of the wall, then gradually they slipped down into the sand. As they gulped their last breath, they faded into oblivion, then as the sand was going over their heads the air supply above had been cut off, but to their surprise they cold breathe.

After a few seconds, the sinking stopped and they were left in a new dimension, they had entered a new world. As they were

81

looking round them, they could only see thick sand in front of their faces. A weird sensation came over both of them, like a tingling feeling all over their bodies, then they fell unconscious and slipped into a sleep state. They had now entered a three-dimensional oblivion, and as the stage two process was starting their bodies were being put through a kind of skin diffusing process.

When the two of them saw this starting, they shouted out, "No, God help us please", then as they suddenly opened their eyes they were amazed to find themselves still in the sand. Dr Arnold said, "What has happened?"

Dr Hines replied "I think it was a dream."

"Now what shall we do? We are still stuck in this god-forsaken rut," said Doctor Arnold.

Then as he felt down at his side, he found something sharp and spiky. He budged it to one side, and they both went accelerating downwards.

The gravitational pull was too much for their bodies, they became paralyzed, disoriented and unbalanced. Then suddenly the accelerating stopped, and they floated down to the ground below and set foot on the floor. Then as Doctor Arnold stood up, still drowsy, he looked up and saw the inscription, "Archway to Hell". As they looked up and saw the sign, they said, "What could have made these inscriptions?"

Doctor Arnold said, "I don't know, but judging the state of it, it must be pre-isolation stage, because the letters on the sign are nearly worn out."

Then as they walked underneath the sign, a voice spoke. "Who are you to venture into my domain? I am Lucifer, who are you?"

"We are doctors from the Egyptology centre."

"Silence, this is my domain."

Then suddenly out from the walls came a strange mist. It did not seem to flow naturally. As it got closer, the two doctors still looking at it, from nowhere came a collection of mutants.

The voice came up again, saying, "Go into the mist both of you. If you don't, I will banish you to the far reaches of hell, even worse than this."

Then as they set foot into the realms of the unknown, all they heard was a scream of laughter. "We have you now," shouted the voices from the mist. Then as the doctors were looking round in fright, all they saw was a line of dead souls, walking in a straight line, coming towards them. Doctor Hines ran screaming towards them, this had the effect of dispersal and made them disoriented. When Doctor Arnold saw this he could not believe his eyes. He shouted as well and ran towards the scattered souls, then as he caught up with his colleague he said, "How did you know?"

"I don't know," she said, "I must have panicked.

"Well, it did the trick, whatever you did."

Then as they turned around the mist was gone, it was nowhere to be seen. As they walked on, everything around them was quite unnatural looking, even the rocks on the walls bore the tell-tale signs of evil. Then as they were passing another of these rocks, a piece moved on its own, so the two doctors went over for a closer look. To their horror, it was human, it shouted out, "Help me, please!" then with that statement the human in the rocks just exploded. Doctor Hines screamed in anger, then she said, "What could have done this?"

"The devil himself."

"Oh my God, help us in our need."

With that, a book dropped from the roof above them.

Then as the doctor bent down to pick up the book from the floor, she slowly read the title, and turned towards Doctor Arnold, saying in a soft voice, "Come here, I have something strange to show you."

Doctor Arnold ran towards her as she turned around with her back to him. He tapped her on the shoulder and said, "What have you found then?"

As she turned round, the doctor felt a dead chill go up his spine. What emerged in front of his face was the sight of a decomposing body. Doctor Arnold fainted with fright.

When Doctor Arnold came round and opened his eyes, the body had gone and Doctor Hines was nowhere to be seen. Slowly the doctor got up from the floor, and still unbalanced from his fright, he walked on down the corridor of rocks. Then as he ventured a hundred yards down the rock chamber, the weirdest sensation came over him, as though he were being watched from a great height.

Suddenly there was a strange electrical storm, and as the doctor looked up above him he saw the devil's face among the

83

clouds. Then as the both of them were looking at each other eye-to-eye, a scream was heard from behind the wall. The doctor said, "If you touch her, that will be your last."

Suddenly the devil pointed his finger towards the doctor, and as he did so a force came out towards him. His first reaction was stand his ground, but then he had second thoughts and ran for his life. As he was running the wall came alive with screaming voices, all of them saying "Die, die." The force engulfed him, then he was lifted up into the air.

By chance he still had Doctor Hines's old book, which she left when she was taken away. As he opened it and started to read from it, a strange illumination came from above, and out from the book came light. When the doctor saw this light coming from the book, he said, "Who are you?"

"I am your inner being," it said.

Then as the doctor read another line in the book, the force was gone and so was the light, and the doctor hit the ground with a thump. As he got up from the floor the walls started to move in on him. He tried to run, but as he looked for a clear path everywhere was blocked. By now the walls were slowly encircling him, then as he was kneeling in the middle of the rock chamber, he found himself sliding down a sand hole. Then, as he was halfway down, the walls stopped coming and halted.

As the doctor slipped from view, his whole transformation was taking place, in the form of an empty soul. Now this transformation was taking him to a far-off place. This place was hell. Suddenly the doctor was blown through the sealed sand, and into the awaiting sky of redness, floating on a cloud. This cloud was bringing him down to earth, an earth he did not know. By this time he was feeling empty and disillusioned. Then as he was sitting on the cloud, he was thinking back to his past, while the cloud was bringing him to his resting place.

Then out of nowhere the sky began to change, it had mini cyclones mixed with mauve and green blots all over the sky, causing an alteration in the dimension. The doctor said, "This is not normal", then everything went black and his cloud was nowhere to be seen. He heard somebody scream out loud. He shouted out, "Who is that?" but all he got was silence, then his face dropped with disillusion.

He slowly walked a couple of yards in front of him, and

suddenly he came face-to-face with a very old door. Then as if by magic, lights came on, and as the doctor looked around him he found himself amongst an old tribe of people. One of the tribespeople said, "Who are you? Are you the chosen one?"

The doctor said to him, "Do you want me to be him?"

"Yes," said the tribesman.

Then suddenly the door opened. The voice of the devil was heard, saying, "Did you think you had seen the last of me?"

"No," said the doctor.

Then the doctor shouted out, "Let the forces of good and evil commence battle!" When the tribesmen heard this they started to chant and scream.

The devil let out a gale which took the doctor off his feet and swept him into the rocks. As the doctor went smashing into the rocks, a puff of smoke followed his entrance, then as the smoke settled onto the floor, a big hole was seen in the middle of the rocks. Then as a thunderbolt came towards the doctor, something happened. In midstream, an archway appeared out of nowhere. Then as the thunderbolt hit the archway it was deflected on to the devil.

The devil was sent reeling, it had weakened him, due to the force and pressure of all the electrical field which had been expelled. Then as the doctor came out of the hole that he was in and jumped onto the floor, he could see all the tribesmen kneeling to him and chanting. They were saying, "The chosen one has saved us, we are free of him, pray to the holy one, he has freed us!"

Then as the doctor heard this he looked round. The devil was only partially wounded. Then as his eyes slid open, a red beam of light came hurtling towards the archway and smashed through it. As the doctor saw this he quickly dived out of the way. He heard a bang, then as he looked up he saw the remains of the hole.

Then, as he picked himself off the floor, where all the scattered rocks had fallen, he was amazed to find himself back inside the tomb, and there was Doctor Hines, safe and sound. Doctor Arnold said, "How did I get here?"

The other doctor said, "You just materialized out of nowhere."

"Where have you been all this time?"

"I was taken when I was reading that book."

Then as the doctor looked down at his hand, he found to his horror that the book had gone, and so was the archway which had saved his life. Had that been the final conflict, or was it the start? He noticed that the hole was healing itself. He put his hand up to feel the light which was healing the hole. Then as he did so, a strange feeling came over him as though he were being reborn. Suddenly, the healing light reflected off the hole, bounced on to the doctor, and his whole dimension started to alter out of all recognition.

Then as the light engulfed him he found his whole body was alight with stars, and a breath of fresh air streamed through him, causing all his hair to stand on end, and his skin to pull outwards, bending as the light was hitting it. As the doctor looked down at this strange phenomenon he was ecstatic with emotion, then gradually the fresh air sped around him making a vapour coil. Then these strange things flying around him changed for the worse, creating and deforming. As he felt this, a sharp pain hit him all over his inner body, making him scream out with anxiety and fear. The doctor said, "Why are you doing this to me?"

Then the voice of the pain said, "This is what you get for killing my friend the devil, and for wounding the wall."

A scream went up saying, "Leave him alone!"

It was his colleague, Doctor Hines, who was holding up a piece of rock. She shouted to it, "Let him go, or face the consequences!"

When the light-pain heard this, it began to laugh out loud. She threw the rock into it.

The impact was felt a long way away, even the rocks around the tomb vibrated with the pressure. Then suddenly a big bang was heard beneath the floor, and a giant obelisk came through the sand. It pierced the floor like a sharp point, then as it stood in its full glory, the doctor looked up at it in total surprise and amazement. Then as the doctor went over to it, he tried to communicate with it, and as he ventured near it he felt a godly wind go straight through him, like a reborn soul.

This wind touched his inner soul, the doctor was left breathless. The obelisk was metamorphosing in front of his eyes, with a strange effect. Tons of mildew were leaking out of it, and seeping over the edge of the obelisk, creating a lava flow of some extent. When the doctor saw this he was anticipating a change, very soon, then it slowly changed form. It was incredible, the doctor was watching every step.

The top half of the obelisk broke open and fell to the ground, making a vibrating noise which was heard around the tomb. Then suddenly there emerged a gruesome sight, a creature with eight horns sticking out of its head. Then as it emerged fully, the creature spoke saying, "I am the creature of the night, you have been tampering with things that you know nothing about."

A barrage of meteors emerged out of its hand and headed towards the lonely doctor who had no defence. But he took out the old book from his back pocket. Then as the creature saw the book in the doctor's hand, he had second thoughts, so he deflected the flying meteors away from him. The doctor heard the meteors go smashing into the rocks one by one, then slowly he started to read the text.

As he did so, he could feel a power building up, and as he read the next line, his hands started to vibrate and shake about, then his voice shook as he was reading the revelations. Then to his surprise, a volley of shots rang out from all quarters of the tomb and from the old obelisk itself. Suddenly the creature screamed out, "Don't say another word!" The doctor read the last paragraph of the revelations. Then everything went quiet.

Then the creature looked down at him and said, "This is going to be your last, so brace yourselves for a collision. This time there will be no turning back." A shower of dust fell to the ground from the top of the tomb, and scattered on the ground leaving a vast layer of petals, face up on the floor.

Then suddenly out of the floor came his lady friend Doctor Hines, wearing a strange garment out of the pre-gothic era. Then as she turned to him, she gave him a sign. Doctor Arnold said, "What does this mean? Is it a sign from God or another of the devil's tricks?"

"Be calm, all is well," she said. "Go into the light, for the light holds the key."

"Go into the light? Why, that's where the creature is!"

"Yes, be brave, all is well," she said.

Then to his surprise, he felt himself being lifted up off his feet, and being directed towards the creature. When he saw what was happening he panicked and started to shout for his life. Then as he went into the creature's domain, the doctor saw a beam of light at the end of the tunnel which was in front of him. A strong wind came up, its force so powerful that it blew him through to another world which was waiting for him on the other side.

This other side was his own world. Or was it? As the doctor looked up, all he saw was a vast tunnel. Then as the creature opened his mouth, the doctor shouted "NO! NO!", then by magic the creature was no more to be seen. This was the end of the two doctors' story. Suddenly the book said, "You have not seen the last of me."

"Help us! This tradition must be stopped!" said the doctor.